THE SECRET LIFE OF AN INSTA-BADDIE

JAI LOVE

THE
SECRET
LIFE
OF AN
INSTA-BADDIE

Title: The Secret Life of an Insta-Baddie

Copyright © 2020 by Jai Love. All rights reserved.

Author: Jai Love

ISBN No: 9780578785097

LCCN No: 2020921497

Editing/Typesetting: 21st Street Urban Editing & Publishing Group

Behind every picture there is a story to tell.

CHAPTER 1

eiko Kei is the name that I go by on social media, but my real name is Kei'na Konners. I remember when I had hundreds of followers, and now I have over eight million followers on Instagram. I've come a long way, and my looks made all of this possible.

Having the right connections, being consistent with posting sexy pictures, keeping up with my looks, and oh, I forgot to mention, sucking and fucking on rich niggas has me living the glamorous life. My smooth caramel complexion, brown almond-shaped eyes, full juicy pink lips, curly jet-black shoulder-length hair, perky 38 C size titties, a small waist, and an ass so fat, make heads turn when I step into a room.

I won't say that living a glamorous life is easy, but by looking at my social media, no one would know what really went on behind closed doors. I look like the happiest person, like I have a perfect life with no worries in the world, and I intend for it to stay that way. As long as the money, the designer shit, exotic trips, and all of the perks of being a popular IG model don't go away, I'll do all that I can to make sure that no one finds out that I live a double life.

I'm really not hurting for money, but I must say, I'm addicted to money and will do anything to get it. I love flossing my money; it brings nothing but fame. Fame should have been my middle name. Every morning when I wake up in my luxury high-rise condo located in downtown Los Angeles, I know that I cannot go back to being broke, and if I have anything to do with it, I never will.

What other twenty-four-year-old owns her own high-rise condo, a white-on-white G Wagon, an unlimited amount of designer clothes, purses and shoes, and has a seven-figure income. I was doing my shit and getting richer and richer. Along with living a life of luxury, there are always haters praying on my downfall. Other IG models are always trying to start beef with me, but all I do is laugh. There is one thing that I am not, and that is I am not scared of no bitch. Yeah, I have fucked niggas that they want, but why be mad at the next bitch. My advice to them would be to step their game up.

Whenever I go to events or host a club, I have to watch my back. Bitches caught me slippin' one time while I was at a party. I got jumped by three females who I was going back and forth with on social media. I don't know why these weak ass bitches couldn't fight me one on one, but I know I fought each one of those bitches with all of my might. After that night, I asked around for some type of private security and was referred to two highly recommended bodyguards, Keith and Joe. These two do not put up with shit from anyone who tries to come for me. They are right by my side whenever I go to a party, a club, event, meeting, or one of my late-night rendezvous. I didn't want too many people to know about my late-night missions, but I trust Joe and Keith and need them to protect me from these crazy ass muthafuckas in the world.

I'm thankful for my two bodyguards; without them, I don't have anyone else in my life besides my best friend, Siana. My dad left our family when I was five years old and my mom turned to drugs and alcohol to help her cope. My sister and I were placed in foster care and when she got adopted two years later, that was the last time I saw her.

Until the day I turned eighteen years old, I bounced around to different foster homes. Each day I had to live my life in survival mode. I had to make it through old dirty ass men touching my young pussy to foster parents beating my ass until I bled whenever I told them that I was getting molested by their husbands, brothers, or family friends. I've been through hell and back. I had to fight to get to where I am today, so I do whatever the fuck I want to get what I want.

Besides Keith and Joe, the only other person I trust with my life is Siana. She is the only real friend that I have. Even though we are complete opposites, I love her like a sister. Siana is the color of brown sugar, with a set of eyes that matches her brown skin tone. She has straight brown hair that flows down to the middle of her back and a body that some would consider slim-thick. Unlike me, Siana hates social media and prefers to live a private life. I could never understand why, but hey, to each their own. There were plenty of occasions where I tried to create social media accounts for her because I knew she would be the hottest thing on the internet, besides me of course. Each time I tried, she put a stop to it. Siana did not like me posting her picture on my page, so after so many attempts, I finally gave up.

She's a videographer for a popular television company which is the perfect job for her. She loves being behind the scenes or behind the camera. I can't imagine not having Siana around; she has talked me out of many fucked up situations. She is the sane one while I, on the other hand, am considered the wild one. Once in a while, I can convince her to attend some of the hottest clubs or celebrity parties with me, but most of the time, she declines. Truth is, I only ask her to come because I know that once I have a few drinks in my system, I can turn into a loose cannon. When Siana is around, she will drag my ass out of there with the quickness. Other than that, I don't invite her out as much anymore because she will literally sit in a corner somewhere the whole night. When she's not acting like a little Ms. Boring Daisy, she's getting attention from niggas, and I need all the attention to be on me. I'm the life of the muthafuckin' party. Don't get me wrong, I love my best friend, but I do get a little jealous when the niggas that I want choose her over me because she wouldn't even know how to handle them. Lucky for me, she never gives out her number and if a nigga gives her his number, she throws it away the first chance she gets. I snatch it up fast if the nigga fits all of my qualifications. Call me thirsty, I don't give a fuck. I just know how to go after whatever the fuck I want.

Siana claims that she doesn't have time for a relationship right now, but I think she's still hurt over her ex. That dumb ass nigga cheated on her with his homeboy's mama. Siana found out when his homeboy came to their house to confront him. He told Siana all about the text messages between her boyfriend and his mama that he read on his mama's phone. I made sure I got his ass back for it though.

Siana still doesn't even know about it to this day. I had a couple of hood niggas I know beat the fuck out of him one night when he was leaving the club. I was sure she would lecture me for doing that, but I did it for her and I don't feel bad about it at all.

CHAPTER 2

"Yes!" I shouted as my eyes rolled all the way back in my head.

The way this man slurped my pussy from my throbbing clit all the way to my asshole while I was bent over, back arched and ass tooted in the air, I couldn't do anything but bite into the sheets and grind my wet pussy and ass all over his face.

"Shit... this pussy tastes good, Keiko," he said as his long snake tongue entered my pussy.

"Mmhm... Please... Mmhm... Don't stop... Mmhm," I begged between moans.

My body started to feel hot as an orgasm built. I backed my pussy into his face with so much force, and he wasn't missing a beat.

"Agh! Fuck!" I screamed, and my whole body was shaking uncontrollably.

My juices flowed out of my pussy and down my legs. His wet tongue licked all of my juices from my legs and then back up to my pussy. I collapsed on the bed. My whole body was still shaking from cumming so hard.

"You need to give me my money and leave," I said once my heart rate went back to normal.

I slowly turned around to face him. He had a confused look painted on his face.

"What the fuck do you mean I need to give you money?" he stared at me, waiting for my answer.

"Nigga, when you slid in my DM you knew what it was. You claimed that you had all this money. Now run me my fucking money!" I shouted, starting to feel annoyed.

"Bitch, I'm not giving yo hoe ass shit!"

He grabbed his keys off the dresser and walked toward the door. I quickly jumped off the bed and got in his face.

"If you don't give me my muthafuckin' money, I swear you will get your ass beat as soon as you walk out this door."

"Fuck you!"

He opened the door and slammed it shut. I quickly ran to grab my cell phone to text a code to Joe to let him know that I needed him to handle that nigga. If he would've given me my money, he would be walking out of here happy that a bitch like me even allowed him to taste this sweet juicy pussy. Now he was going to go home pissed off after getting an ass whooping from Joe.

I went back to bed and closed my eyes until I heard someone yelling downstairs. I jumped up and rushed to the floor-to-ceiling windows. I smiled when I realized my bodyguard was beating his ass something serious. Melo was laid out on the ground while Joe went into his pockets and pulled out something. I stood in front of the window long enough to see Melo look up at the window and said, "Bitch, watch your back."

I smiled, flicked him my middle finger, and backed away from the window. I heard a knock, and I knew it had to be Joe at the door. I opened the door and Joe held out his hand and opened it.

"Ten fucking dollars! This is all that muthafucka had in his pockets," Joe said as he shook his head from side-to-side.

"Broke ass."

I snatched the money out of Joe's hand. He laughed and walked away. I closed the door and went back to bed. I was pissed off, that nigga Melo tried to play me, but I was still horny. I spread my legs wide open and rubbed on my fat clit. My pussy was still wet from my juices and Melo's spit. I used the wetness to coat my clit and went to work. I rubbed on my clit and finger fucked myself until I had another orgasm. My sheets were soaking wet. Too tired to move, I fell asleep right in my wet spot.

CHAPTER 3

$\mathcal{I}$ woke up and thought about last night. I can't believe that nigga Melo, but whatever, at least I was able to get some bomb head from him. I was happy that I decided to book a hotel suite last minute; Lord knows, I don't need his crazy ass knowing where I reside.

I got out of bed to do my morning stretch and get ready for the day. I was going to the mall to do a little shopping for some outfits to wear for my upcoming events. I decided to wear some black leggings, my black and red Supreme hoodie, and my all-black Balenciaga sneakers. I will be shopping all day, and want to be comfortable while I do damage in these stores. I usually get all dressed up, wear heels and do all the extra shit when I go shopping anticipating who might see me out in public. Today, I'm making an exception because a bitch is tired as fuck. I'm not in the mood to drive, so I hired a driver for the day. I checked my appearance one more time in the mirror until I was satisfied with my look. I grabbed my Birkin bag and headed down to the lobby to wait for my driver.

* * *

I GOT INVITED TO A POOL PARTY FOR ALL OF THE POPULAR
social media influencers this weekend at a mansion in
Hollywood Hills. I'm looking forward to this party. There
will be some big ballers in the building and I need to be in
the center of it all. Maybe I'll invite Siana, but I doubt
she'll even come. While I shop, I will try to come up with a
way to convince Siana to tag along with me to this pool
party.

As I walked around the mall, I started to feel hungry so
I stopped at one of the restaurants to order a shrimp and
veggie bowl. While I ate my food, I checked my emails.
One email stood out to me the most because it was from a
very high-end company named Crystals Galore.

This clothing company is known for its fancy clothing
pieces covered in crystals. I own one of their pieces. It is a
pink silk dress with beautiful pink crystals precisely placed
all over the form fitting, knee length dress. One of the guys
I used to fuck around with bought it for me when he took
me on a shopping spree. The dress cost $40,000, and he
gladly handed over his black card after I told him what I
would do to him later that night.

I stopped daydreaming and continued reading the
email. The email stated that the owners of the company
would like to meet with me. I was surprised. For most of the
jobs that I booked, I always went through the company's
representative but never had direct contact with the owner.
Shit, I didn't even know the owners of Crystals Galore, but
for the price of their pieces, they had to have major bank.
At the end of the email, there was a contact number, so I
quickly dialed the number.

"Thank you for calling Crystals Galore. This is Ana

speaking, how may I direct your call?" the lady said in the squeakiest voice I have ever heard.

I removed the phone from my ear and looked at the screen trying not to laugh.

"Hi, my name is Keiko Kei and I received an email from your company." I tried my best to sound professional.

"Ms. Kei, please hold. I will transfer your call over to our social media department," Ana said, and shortly after, I heard that boring ass elevator music playing in my ear.

After waiting for two minutes, I heard someone come on the line.

"Ms. Keiko Kei, thank you for returning my call. I am Ed Broski, and I am Mrs. Galore's personal assistant. Mr. and Mrs. Galore would love to meet you for dinner to discuss a business offer." Ed paused and waited for my response.

Nigga, of course I'm interested. I was thinking, but instead I said, "I would love to meet with Mr. and Mrs. Galore. When would you like to schedule this meeting, sir?" I responded, sounding proper as fuck.

"When are you available?" Ed quickly asked.

I have a busy schedule coming up, so I thought that the sooner I met with them, the better it would be for me. "Actually, I'm available tonight."

I had the biggest smile on my face. I couldn't wait to find out what the fuck Mr. and Mrs. Galore wanted with little ol' me.

"Wonderful! I will get back to you with more information within the next hour, Ms. Kei." Ed sounded happy.

"Okay, thank you, Mr. Broski," I said before hanging up.

I finished my shrimp veggie bowl and continued shopping. Now, I had to get an outfit for tonight.

* * *

As soon as I walked into the blinged out boutique, the emerald green body-con backless dress caught my attention. This would look amazing on me and the color would match my skin-tone perfectly. I looked for my size and grabbed the dress off the rack. I walked to the back of the boutique to the fitting room. There was a chandelier hanging from the ceiling, a large mirror that covered the whole wall, and a plush hot pink chaise lounge chair. This fitting room was right up my alley, it was very lavish.

I tried on the dress, and I instantly fell in love. It fit me like a glove, and I know it would be suitable for the occasion. I have the perfect gold and emerald green heels that will go well with the dress. I gave the dress one more look from all angles before I changed back into my regular clothes and exited the fitting room.

"Your total is four-hundred dollars. Would you like to pay with cash, or will you be using a card?" the skinny sales associate asked while she looked me up and down.

"Cash."

I handed her four, crisp, one hundred dollar bills. She put my dress in a hot pink bag along with my receipt. I took the bag from her and left the store. I felt her eyes on me as I walked out. I slowly turned around and gave her a smirk. The bitch probably thought I couldn't pay for the dress. That is what I experience every time I step foot into one of those uppity boutiques. I went to a couple more stores before I decided to call it a day. I was drained, and I needed to get some much-needed sleep.

An hour later, right on the dot, Mr. Broski called me back to confirm the details for my meeting with Mr. and

Mrs. Galore tonight. He gave me a Bel-Air address and my pussy got wet when I thought about the dollars.

* * *

I DROVE UP TO THE WEST GATE ENTRANCE TO ENTER BEL-Air. Don't get me wrong, I've been around plenty of big ballers, but this is on a whole different level. I gained access and drove to the address that Ed sent me. The mansions were hidden behind trees so there wasn't much sight-seeing. I didn't know what to expect in this meeting, but I tried to mentally prepare myself for anything. I drove until I arrived at a large gold gate. I pressed the buzzer and seconds later, the large gate slowly opened up. I drove in after the gate opened wide enough for me to enter.

When the mansion came into full view, I was in awe. I have never seen anything like it. Their mansion was all gold and there was a large gold fountain placed in the middle of the circular driveway.

I stepped out of my G Wagon, straightened out my dress, fluffed out my curls a little and walked up to the front door. As soon as I was getting ready to press the doorbell, the door opened. There stood who I assumed to be Mr. and Mrs. Galore.

"Ms. Keiko Kei! It is a pleasure to have you over for dinner. Please, come in." Mrs. Galore didn't even wait for me to respond before she pulled me into their home.

"Good evening, Mr. and Mrs. Galore. I am honored to be here."

I looked at them and smiled. I noticed that Mr. Galore didn't say a word, but he couldn't keep his eyes off of me. Mrs. Galore tried to be low-key when she gave him a nudge on his side.

"Welcome to our home, Ms. Kei," Mr. Galore finally snapped out of his trance and greeted me.

"Thank you, and please call me Keiko."

I tried to keep my composure. I was amazed; the inside of their home was even grander than the outside. I wanted to take a tour of their home, but a bitch needed to chill the fuck out.

"Okay, Keiko. Please follow us this way."

I followed Mr. and Mrs. Galore into a room that could fit four large apartments. Everything in their home was white and gold. They definitely had good taste. We walked until we reached a long pearly white and gold dining room table that could easily seat forty people, or more. They had a variety of food placed on the table. There was Italian food, Mexican, Chinese, and even fried chicken. All of this shit couldn't only be for three people.

"We had no knowledge of your favorite dish, so we ordered a little bit of everything, Keiko." Mrs. Galore looked at the food and then looked at me with a slight smile.

"Wow," I was speechless. "This was a sweet gesture. Thank you."

I didn't know what else to say, *but I know I need them to adopt a bitch right the fuck now*, I thought as I smiled at the couple.

"Come on, let us eat," Mr. Galore said as he made sure his wife and myself were seated before he took his seat at the head of the table.

The food was looking and smelling good. I dived right in. I started with the lobster and crab pasta. I glanced up and Mr. Galore had that look again. I knew what the fuck that look meant, but I couldn't believe he was staring at me like that with his wife sitting right in front of him.

"Keiko, as you already know we would like to do business with you. We are coming out with a new clothing line, and we would love for you to be the face of our collection. It will consist of bodysuits and two-piece matching sets. Mr. Galore and I think that you are the perfect person for the job. You are absolutely stunning and that beautiful brown skin would look exquisite in our new pieces."

They both stared at me, waiting for an answer.

"Hell ye... I mean, yes, I would love to be the face of your new collection."

I was beyond ecstatic that I was going to be a part of the Crystals Galore team, and I was so ready to start. This would open up more doors for me, give me so much more exposure, and I'll be getting my bag.

"Great!" Mr. and Mrs. Galore said in unison. They both looked at each other and smiled.

I continued munching on my food.

"There is one more thing," Mrs. Galore said.

I stopped chewing my food and gave her my undivided attention.

"Can my husband have you while I watch?"

It got so quiet in the room you could hear a pin drop. *I knew this shit was too good to be true.* Rich, freaky deaky, White people are always up to some type of weird shit.

I knew exactly what the fuck she meant, but I still asked.

"I don't think I quite understand, can he have me in what way, Mrs. Galore?"

"My husband first heard about you from his friend in the industry, and when he showed me your photo, I was fascinated. He confessed that he was having sexual thoughts about you, and I completely understood why. When the perfect opportunity came for us to meet you, we jumped on it right away. Please allow my husband to have sex with you.

If you agree, we promise that you will not be disappointed and you will be highly compensated, along with the business deal that we are offering you."

They anxiously waited to hear my response.

Hearing that I would be 'highly compensated' instantly made me ready to get this shit started. I looked over at Mr. Galore.

"Yes, you can have me."

I swear this man started to drool. My appetite was gone, and I was ready to make my money. I was still shocked that this is the type of shit they were into. Don't get me wrong, they looked to be in their mid-fifties, and they looked good for their age, but I would have never expected this from them. I had never fucked a White man before, and I was used to picking the dudes I wanted to have sex with from social media, but never no shit like this. This will definitely be one for the books.

The Galores were cheesing so hard I couldn't help but smile as well.

"Keiko, before we start would you mind signing this contract?"

She handed me the contract which stated that everything that happens in the home is confidential, and if I violate the contract, there will be monetary consequences to pay. I looked up and she had a pen ready for me.

"No problem."

I had no problem signing the contract because I did not want anyone to find out about this either. I signed the contract and handed it back to her. Mr. Galore stood up, took his wife's hand as well as my hand, and escorted us to another room.

There was an indoor pool with a waterfall. The lights were dimly lit, and there were candles everywhere. It smelled like honey and vanilla. There were cabana style beds surrounding the pool. This pool room was absolutely breathtaking. Yeah, these muthafuckas were a different type of rich. Mr. Galore escorted us to one of the cabanas and told me to undress. It was crazy that suddenly, he wanted to talk. Mrs. Galore had done most of the talking since I arrived at the house, and now he was demanding shit.

I did as I was told and stepped out of my dress but left my Gucci heels on. Mrs. Galore removed her gold silk dress and left her heels on as well. Next, Mr. Galore took off his white suit, and dress shoes. I must say, I was shocked to see how fit their bodies were and that this old White man had a decent size pink dick. That made things that much easier. If I'm going to make money doing this, I might as well enjoy it.

They both stared at me seductively, and all I could see when I stared back were dollar signs. Mrs. Galore went to sit on a chair that was placed next to the cabana bed and Mr. Galore sat me on the bed.

"Spread your legs and let me see your cunt."

I almost burst out in laughter. *Did this nigga just say cunt?* This is going to be a long night. I spread my legs, and he slowly went down to my pussy and put his pointy ass nose in it as he deeply inhaled. His eyes rolled to the back of his head as he sniffed the fuck out of my pussy like I was some type of drug. He put my legs back until he was face-to-face with my bootyhole and did the same thing. His nose tickled my hole as he sniffed my asshole. *This shit is weird as fuck,* but I let the man continue doing his thing. I turned to look at Mrs. Galore and her eyes were glued on us. I wondered how she felt about her husband inhaling my scent.

"Oh Keiko, this sweet Black cunt."

Here this nigga go again. I had to snap out of it and go along with this shit.

"Yes, Mr. Galore. You like this sweet cunt?"

I'm too good at this, I thought.

"Give it to me," he said, barely above a whisper.

He slowly got up and reached for a condom. His eyes roamed all over my body as he slid the condom on. He came back to the area where I laid on the bed and positioned himself in front of me. His dick poked at my hole until it slid in.

"Grrr..."

He was making growling noises as he pumped in and out of my pussy. Mr. Galore's pink dick was starting to feel good. Not the best I've ever had, but it would do for now. I turned my head to the side to see what Mrs. Galore was doing and her hand was between her legs, fingers going to work. I smiled as I placed my legs behind my head. This position drove Mr. Galore wild. He started fucking me faster.

"Aaahh!" he shouted out as his whole body stiffened as warm cum filled the condom.

Seconds later, I heard Mrs. Galore moaning. I looked at her and she looked like she was having a seizure. I will probably go to hell for this, but I wanted to laugh at the way that she looked. It must've been a normal thing because it did not phase Mr. Galore at all, he continued getting dressed. I was ready to get my money and get the fuck up out of here. Even though I was in love with their mansion, I needed to get away from these crazy ass White folks. I couldn't wait to find out how much money they were giving me. I don't know why I didn't ask before I did it. I just heard, 'highly compensated' and was ready to spread eagle for a muthafucka.

"Keiko, you have made my husband a very happy man and I absolutely enjoyed the show. I will have my assistant email you the contract for the business offer and we look forward to having you on our team."

This woman went right back to business mode and was acting like her husband wasn't just sniffing the fuck out of my pussy and asshole.

"Thank you, Mr. and Mrs. Galore. I look forward to joining your team."

We walked back toward the front of the house and I couldn't help but take in the beauty of their home one more time. When we arrived at the front door, Mr. Galore handed me a folded piece of paper, which looked like a check. I got excited. I was ready to run to my truck to see how much that fuck session was worth. We said our good-byes and I was out of there. I waited until I left their premises to look at the check. I almost crashed when I saw the amount. Mr. and Mrs. Galore wrote me a check for eighty thousand dollars. That was the easiest and most money I had ever received for fucking, and I was elated.

Like YG said, this pussy got power. I drove my ass home with the biggest smile on my face.

CHAPTER 4

I woke up feeling like I was on cloud nine. I was still flabbergasted that I made eighty thousand for fucking another woman's husband while she watched. I must say, last night was a success.

I need to get my ass up out of this bed. I have emails to check, phone meetings, and sponsor posts that I need to work on. The earlier I start, the sooner I can see what kind of trouble I can get into tonight.

An email from Crystals Galore caught my attention. It was the contract for the business deal. I opened the attachment in the email and looked over the contract. I didn't care what else I had going on when it came to taking the deal. I would be working with the company by modeling in their fashion shows, doing sponsored posts, and attending a few events for three months. This is a piece of cake and nothing that I wasn't already used to. What I'm not used to is the amount they were offering me. For three months of my time, the Galores are offering five hundred thousand dollars. I would be a fool if I didn't sign this contract. I signed the forms electronically and sent them over to Mrs. Galore's assistant, Ed. He responded with an email that simply said, *Welcome to our team, Ms. Kei.*

* * *

I WAS STILL ON CLOUD NINE FROM ALL OF THAT EASY MONEY that I made with the Galores. I was on my way to the bank to deposit my check and visit Siana. Later tonight, I was trying to get lit and have another wild night.

I walked into the bank and all eyes were on me. I wore a two-piece, hot pink, pants set, with hot pink Gucci sneakers to match. My fake curly ponytail and large hoop earrings went well with my fit.

As I stood in line, I could feel the guy behind me eyes roaming all over my body. I slowly turned around to catch him in the act and he didn't even try to hide that he was staring. I couldn't help but stare into this fine chocolate man's eyes. *Damn, he is so fucking handsome.* I turned my ass back around when I heard the bank teller say next in line.

"Hi, I would like to deposit a check."

I slid the check and my ID into the glass opening. The woman paused and looked at me suspiciously. I was annoyed just that quick, but I understood the process of depositing any amount over ten thousand dollars. After the currency transaction report form was completed, I exited the building.

I walked out of the bank and ran right into Mr. Hand-some Chocolate.

"Took you long enough, luv. A nigga was out here burning up waiting for your sexy ass."

His smooth ass didn't take his eyes off of me not even for a second.

"Did I tell your ass to be waiting for me out here?" I challenged him as I placed my hands on my hips.

On the inside, I was melting. This man was so damn good looking. He let out a little laugh and took my small hand into his large hand.

"I like that slick mouth of yours. I'm Samir, and you are?"

He gave me the brightest smile, and I couldn't hold back my smile any longer.

"Nice to meet you, Samir. My name is Kei'na."

I done gave this man my government name. I had to be trippin'. He was still holding onto my hand and I was ready to give it up to this nigga right there in the parking lot. Shit, the way he was holding my hand made me ready to have his baby. I had to snap out of that shit, real quick. No man had ever made me feel like this.

"Nice to meet you as well, Kei'na. If you are free tonight, I would love to take you out?" Samir patiently waited for my answer.

"Give me your number and if my schedule frees up, I will give you a call."

I was blushing hard, but I tried my best to stay calm.

"Sounds good."

I handed him my phone so that he could store his number. Shortly after that, we parted ways. I didn't care what I had planned for the night, I was going to be with Samir.

* * *

I MADE IT TO SIANA'S HOUSE AND I TEXTED HER TO LET HER know that I was outside. I left the spare key that she gave me in my condo, so I couldn't let myself in. She texted me back and told me that the door was open. I grabbed my mini Gucci purse, made my way to her front door and walked in.

Siana had Jhene Aiko blasting through her speakers. She was nowhere in sight, so I walked around the house trying to find her. I heard the shower on in one of her bathrooms and the door was slightly ajar.

"Si..."

I could barely get Siana's name out as I peered through the clear shower door and stared at a buff ass man the color of cinnamon taking a shower in Siana's home. I was stuck in my position just staring at this fine man. Once he finally realized there was someone standing there, he grabbed a washcloth and covered his dick. It was too late, though. I had already seen that big Mandingo looking dick hanging down between his legs.

As if on cue, Siana popped up. "Kei'na! Come on!" She grabbed my arm and closed the bathroom door behind her.

"Siana, who the fuck is that big dick having nigga in your bathroom?" I looked at her with a confused look on my face.

"Well, hello to you too, Kei'na," Siana said in a sarcastic tone.

I didn't even bother responding to her sarcastic ass. She finally noticed the serious look on my face as I waited for her to explain.

"That's Zay. I met him at my job three months ago."

"Okay, and what is his ass doing butt-naked in your bathroom?"

She was not answering the real question that I wanted to know.

"Kei'na, not that it's any of your business, but Zay and I are dating. It was very much unexpected, because you know I was not ready to date anyone, no time soon. Zay just seems different, but we are taking it slow."

Siana was smiling so damn hard. I was a bit jealous, but I couldn't let Siana know that.

"Damn, bestie, so this nigga knocking the brakes off that pussy, huh?" I stared at Siana with envy in my eyes.

"Actually, we haven't had sex yet," Siana said.

I stood there speechless with my mouth open and my bottom lip hanging down to the floor. "Girl, what the fuck do you mean y'all haven't had sex yet? Also, why am I just hearing about this man?"

"Kei, everyone is not like you. I prefer to wait until I'm ready, and he has no problem with it. I haven't talked to you about him because lately, we haven't really had time to catch up."

"Whatever Siana, if I was you, I would've been gave up the pussy to that fine ass man," I laughed and playfully punched her arm.

"Trust me, I know," she joked, playfully hitting me back.

Zay walked into the living room fully dressed. He walked over to Siana and gently kissed her forehead. Siana gave him a girlish smile and grabbed his hands. They acted like I wasn't in the room, so I cleared my throat to help bring them back to reality.

"Oh Zay, this is my best friend, Kei'na." Then she looked over at me. "Kei'na, meet Zay."

"Nice to meet you, Kei'na."

Zay walked over to me and extended his hand. I shook his hand, and I almost apologized for walking in on him while he took a shower, but I decided not to because I wasn't sorry at all. Shit, I didn't know he was at Siana's house.

"Nice to meet you as well, Zay."

He quickly let go of my hand and his attention went back to Siana.

"I'm going to head out, beautiful. I'll call you later."

Zay gave her a quick kiss on the lips and gave me a quick wave goodbye as he walked out of the door.

"Does he have any brothers?" I asked Siana as soon as I heard the front door close.

Siana rolled her eyes. "No, he's an only child."

I was over this little girl-talk with my best friend, but I was going to stick around a little while longer. I couldn't suppress the fact that I was feeling slightly jealous of Siana and Zay. We continued to catch up for an hour, and I convinced her to come with me to the pool party this weekend. After saying no four times, she said yes just to shut me up.

I left her house with so many thoughts running through my mind. I needed to clear my head, so I decided to hit up Samir's handsome ass and take him up on that offer to take me out.

* * *

SAMIR AND I DECIDED TO MEET AT THE SANTA MONICA Pier. Usually, I would pick an expensive place for a date, but tonight I wanted to be on some chill shit. I waited in my truck until Samir sent me a text letting me know that he arrived.

Tonight, I kept my outfit simple, a black mini skirt, black turtleneck thong body-suit and my black Christian Dior sandals. My mind drifted to Siana, and I was still feeling a little envious. I couldn't understand why. I had it all.

My phone buzzed, interrupting my thoughts. It was Samir letting me know that he had arrived and was making his way to the entrance of the pier. I grabbed my Christian Dior mini backpack and made my way to Samir.

As I walked up, I couldn't help but admire him. Earlier, I didn't notice his two deep cheek dimples. When we made eye contact, he gave me the biggest smile, showing me his pearly whites. He embraced me in the biggest hug, and for a second, I felt so special.

"Hey beautiful," Samir was cheesing hard as he looked me up and down. "You look amazing Kei'na." He couldn't take his eyes off of me.

"Thank you, Samir. You don't look too bad yourself."

Who was I kidding, this chocolate man was looking fine as fuck. *I think I might be addicted to sex.* As I stood there in front of him, all I was thinking about was what was hanging between his legs.

What a coincidence, Samir was wearing all black too. He wore black jeans, black tee, and black and white Air Jordan 1's. He was looking good enough to eat.

"Thank you, let's walk and get to know each other."

He held onto my hand and we walked toward the arcade. We spent an hour and a half playing games. In a matter of minutes, I learned that we were both competitive which made the date fun. I was starving, so we put a stop to playing the arcade games and went on a hunt for some food. I didn't want to eat a big meal, so we settled for chicken strips and fries.

Sitting on the bench, eating and talking to Samir felt so natural. The jokes flowed continuously, and he made me laugh so much. I had never felt this feeling before, and I liked it a lot. For a split second, I wondered if this is what a real relationship would feel like. We continued to talk, and I told him that I am a popular social media influencer. He wasn't too familiar with what a social media influencer is, so I broke it down for him. He told me that he wasn't on social media and I looked at him like he was crazy. *Everyone is on social media. Well, except for Siana.*

"You are missing out, Samir. Social media is everything."

I stared at him, confused about why he wasn't on social media.

"Nah, luv. Social media ain't for me."

He was dead-ass serious. I decided to drop the conversation because he was sounding like Siana.

"Alright, well I told you what I do for a living. What do you do, Samir?" I anxiously waited for him to tell me that he was making major bank.

"I'm a garbage collector," Samir proudly stated.

I didn't think I heard correctly, so I kept digging for more information. "What exactly is a garbage collector?" I tried not to sound so disappointed.

"I drive trash trucks and collect garbage," he said as he looked at me with a confused expression on his face.

I was turned all the way off. I couldn't seriously deal with a nigga who worked a 9-5. I'm attracted to baller niggas only, and finding out Samir isn't a baller meant this wouldn't be going anywhere. Maybe I will get a quick fuck, and nothing more. I was having a great ass time until he mentioned what he did for a living. What a waste of a fine ass man.

"Oh, I see. That is an interesting job, Samir."

I didn't know what else to say. Honestly, I was ready to end the date, but I for damn sure was going to get my fix before doing so. We walked toward the Ferris wheel. He paid for a ride, and when we made it to the top, I was going to make my move.

"Why are you so quiet now, Kei'na?"

Samir was looking like a sad puppy, and even though I wanted to say, *because I don't fuck with 9-5 niggas,* I held my tongue.

"I'm just taking in this beautiful scenery, that's all."

I gave him a fake smile as the Ferris wheel made it to the top. I massaged his dick through his pants. I was loving what I was feeling as it grew hard.

"Take it out for me."

I was aggressive and I didn't care. Samir hesitated, and I gave him a sad face and he reluctantly did as he was told. When he pulled that long, thick, chocolatey dick out of his pants, I almost fainted. His dick was beautiful. I immediately got mad. This will be the first and last time I fuck him.

I didn't even need to say anything else. I hiked up my skirt a little bit and sat on his raw dick. I couldn't believe that I didn't make this stranger wear a condom, but we didn't have time for that. I needed to cum before this Ferris wheel ride was over.

I had to adjust to his dick size as it filled my stomach. After I got used to his size, I rode that muthafucka like I was in a rodeo. The Ferris wheel started to slowly move again and I rode his dick even faster. My orgasm was coming, and Samir was going to cum soon too. I held onto his neck tightly as I bit into my bottom lip. He gripped my ass and slammed my pussy roughly onto his dick. I tried to slide off of his pole, but I wasn't fast enough. Soon after, I felt my juices and his cum mixing inside of my pussy.

Samir quickly put his dick away, and I rolled my skirt back down as the Ferris wheel came to a complete stop letting us know that our ride was over. We exited the Ferris wheel and made our way back to the parking lot.

Our walk to the parking lot was awkward. I don't know what was running through Samir's mind, but it was probably the same thoughts that I was having. That fuck session was intense as fuck. I had never felt no shit like that while having sex, and to top it off, I allowed this nigga to cum in me.

I couldn't see Samir again. I was not about to get caught up catching deep feelings for a man who wasn't making more than me. Call me shallow, but it's my life and I like what I like. I didn't know exactly what that was on the Ferris wheel, but it was something that I needed to run away from now.

"Kei'na, when can I see you again?"

Samir looked sprung already. As much as I wanted to fall into his arms, I just couldn't do it.

"Um Samir, we will keep in touch." I quickly looked away from him.

"Okay, beautiful. Drive safe and let me know when you make it home," Samir said with a sincere look on his face.

"Alright. Take care, Samir."

I couldn't make eye contact with him. He was perfect, but his 9–5 job wasn't. *Damn, why couldn't he be a baller?* I drove home reminiscing about Samir and myself on that Ferris wheel. My pussy was still throbbing. *I need to forget about Samir, ASAP.*

CHAPTER 5

onight is the pool party, and I'm ready to shake my ass all night long. I'm going to call Siana to make sure her boo'd up ass is still rolling with me.

"Sisi, what up, bestie!" I shouted into the phone.

"Nothing much, Kei. I'm just waking up about to get my day started," Siana said.

"Okay, cool. Are you still coming with me to the pool party tonight?" I asked her, hoping she would say yes.

"Yes, I am. Is it cool if I bring Zay?" Siana immediately got quiet and waited for my response.

"No, it ain't cool, Siana. Why can't we go out alone without a nigga?" I smacked my lips and rolled my eyes. She had killed my mood just that fast.

"Kei, I'm not trying to go back and forth with you right now. I want Zay to come because we are slowly getting closer, and I would really like to see how he acts and adapts to certain environments," Siana tried to explain.

"I guess, bring his ass." I was mad and ready to uninvite Siana.

"Thanks, Kei!"

We said our goodbyes and ended the call.

* * *

I HAD MY OUTFIT LAID OUT AND COULDN'T WAIT TO GET into this skimpy ass bathing suit. I was going to wear a baby blue mesh two-piece bathing suit and my clear jelly sandals. I was ready to head out in the streets with just my bathing suit and sandals on, but I needed to have a cover-up on when I walked to my truck. I pulled out my booty shorts and a baby blue tube top. It wasn't much of a cover-up, but it would do. I put my hair in a high bun with my baby hairs laid and poppin'.

Since Siana was bringing Mr. Zay, we decided to meet at the mansion. Usually, we rode together, so I was slightly irritated with the switch-up, but I was going to do my best to enjoy my night regardless of turning into the third wheel. I needed a nap before getting ready to ensure that my energy level would be high. I was planning to show the fuck out at this pool party.

* * *

SIANA AND I PULLED UP TO THE HOLLYWOOD HILLS mansion at the same time. While she parked her car, I checked my makeup in the mirror and reapplied my Fenty lip gloss. When I was done, I looked through the window to see if Siana and Zay were making their way to me yet.

Zay and Siana were walking toward my truck, and I couldn't help but feel that jealous feeling creeping up on me again. Siana looked amazing. She wore a bright yellow two-piece bathing suit, a sheer short yellow skin tight cover-up dress, and yellow strappy sandals. Zay was looking even better than I remember. He wore yellow swim trunks, a wife beater, and some Gucci slides. Both of them were taking forever to make it to my truck because they were too busy playing around with each other. I rolled my eyes at them and waited for the lovebirds.

"It's about time y'all lovey-dovey asses made it over here."

I looked at them both before turning in the direction of the mansion and leading the way. As soon as we walked into the party, I heard Cisco's "Thong Song" playing, blasting through the large speakers that were placed around the backyard. This was my cue to show out. I handed Siana my bag as I removed my shorts and tube top and started shaking my ass. All of my goodies were on display in this bikini, but that was the least of my worries. I dropped it low and started twerking so hard that my bikini top was sliding up exposing my perky titties. It wasn't like my shit wasn't already showing through this mesh, so I just let it all hang out. I didn't stop twerking until the song ended. I had a large crowd surrounding me cheering me on. I loved having all eyes on me.

The good thing about the influencer party is there were no phones allowed. They collected our phones at the door and placed them into small, color coordinated bags and gave each of us a tag that would allow us to retrieve our phones when we exited.

I adjusted my bathing suit and greeted the people that I recognized in the crowd. There were mostly YouTube and IG influencers in attendance and many of them were popular. I continued mingling with the crowd before walking over to Siana and Zay.

I did a double take when I saw Siana grinding her ass

all over Zay's dick. I know Ms. Goody Two Shoes was not openly dancing in a sexual manner. I gave her a look, and she stopped, whispered something in Zay's ear, and he kissed her forehead and walked away.

"Girl, who the fuck are you, and what did you do to my best friend?" I crossed my arms while I stared at Siana up and down.

"I'm just trying to have fun that's all. Matter-of-fact you should be happy that I'm loosening up a little bit." Siana was giggling like a little kid.

I shook my head at her and told her that I was going to go talk to a YouTube couple that I met a couple months back at an event. I probably should be happy for Siana, but I wasn't used to seeing this side of her so I didn't know how to handle it. Maybe deep down, I wanted to feel the same way Siana was feeling right now. Naw, my focus was on getting my bag and living the glamorous life.

As I talked to the couple, I wasn't really focused on the conversation because I couldn't keep my eyes off of Siana and Zay. They were in the pool tonguing down each other as he gripped her ass. Siana playfully pushed his hands away and got out of the pool. I watched her carefully as she entered the mansion. I assumed she was going to the restroom. I looked back over at Zay and he was walking to the bar. This is the perfect opportunity for me to go see what Mr. Zay is all about. I dismissed myself and walked over to Zay.

"What's up, you enjoying yourself?"

I stood behind Zay close enough for him to feel my breath on the back of his neck. He was caught off guard, and he quickly backed away from me.

"Yes, I am. Siana has made sure of that." He was cheesing so damn hard.

"Yeah, okay. Well, I can show you an even better time."

I moved closer to him and rubbed my titties on his chest.

"Yo..." Zay backed away with both hands raised up in the air.

"Kei, what the fuck are you doing?"

I heard Siana's voice before turning around to face her. If looks could kill, I probably would have dropped down dead right then. I had never seen that look on Siana's face before. Not even when she found out that her ex was cheating. I didn't understand why she was looking at me like she was crazy because of this new nigga she barely knew.

"Just having some harmless fun, Siana."

She was pissing me off and I was close to slapping the shit out of her for screaming at me in front of all these people.

"Bullshit! Kei'na, I don't have shit else to say to you! We're leaving!"

She grabbed Zay's hand and marched toward the exit.

I know this shit is not happening right now. A crowd had built up again around me and this time it wasn't for a good reason. I love attention, but not this type of attention.

"Fuck her!" I shouted as I pushed through the crowd.

I needed to take a minute to myself, so I went straight to the restroom to recollect my thoughts. I wasn't ready to end my night. I was not about to let Siana ruin it. After getting myself together, I walked back outside and acted like nothing happened. I went back to the bar and got myself a cup of Henny and pineapple juice. I was ready to get fucked up and forget about what happened with Siana.

I continued to mingle and network with a few people who I wanted to collaborate with and the whole time, I kept throwing the drinks back, until the dark liquor made a bitch horny as fuck, indicating it was time to stop. I looked around until I spotted my victim for the night. I was familiar with MoneyLongBoii. He was popular on IG and known for flexing all over the Gram. I don't know how he made his money, but the way he was throwing money on the girls who surrounded him by the DJ booth, I wanted some of that action.

I sashayed my ass right over to him and I demanded his attention. I stopped right in front of him, causing the other girls to all pause and look at each other. After realizing that I was not going anywhere, they scattered away leaving MoneyLongBoii and myself standing there, face-to-face.

"Where's my money? You should be throwing that money on me. I'll give you your money's worth."

I got straight to the point. I was hot and ready. I was yearning to cream on a dick and MoneyLongBoii was the perfect candidate for the night.

"The one and only, Keiko Kei. I'll give you everything I have in my hand right now, ma." He was staring me up and down as he licked his lips. "Follow me."

I didn't waste any time. I grabbed the money out of his hands and placed it in my bag. I led him to a secluded garden area I'd seen when I went to the bathroom. It would be the perfect area to get my fuck on.

"You don't play, ma. Let me go grab a condom from my homie right quick and I'll meet you back over here."

He jogged away, and it wasn't even a full two minutes before I saw him quickly jogging back.

"Pull that dick out, let me see what you workin' with."

I looked down watching him closely as he pulled out a skinny looking pencil dick. If I wasn't so horny, I would've left his ass right there in that garden. He could barely fit the large condom, and there was still a lot of room left in the rubber.

I pulled my bikini bottom to the side and he came right over. I was in no mood to talk, so I grabbed his little dick and guided it straight to my hole. As soon as he felt the inside of my gushy pussy, his eyes rolled to the back of his head, and I rolled my eyes unable to feel shit. I couldn't even fake the shit; three minutes later, he was cumming, and I was completely over it.

"You got some bomb ass pussy, ma. We gon' have to do this again."

He removed the condom and pulled up his shorts. I wasn't done with his ass yet, and I for sure was going to cum tonight. Instead of responding to his comment, I laid his ass down on the bright green grass. I placed my now dry pussy right on his full lips.

"Eat this pussy."

I wasn't playing with his ass. He began licking, but it wasn't to my liking. To help speed up the process, I started to grind my pussy all over his face. I was being rough and it was starting to turn me on. Maybe I needed to become a dominatrix. I was definitely going to revisit this idea again. For now, I needed to focus on cumming on this man's face.

MoneyLongBoii had my pussy juice all over his face. My orgasm was building, which caused me to grind harder. His tongue was finally hitting my spot.

"Keep licking this fucking pussy... don't stop licking..."

My cum oozed out of my pussy right onto his lips and dripped down his chin.

"You was tryna suffocate a nigga? I mean, I ain't trippin', but damn. You got that good, ma."

He was looking at me intensely while licking my juices off of his lips.

I was finally ready to leave this party. Despite my little incident with Siana, I was able to connect with a few people, get money and bust a nut. That is always a great night for me.

MoneyLongBoii was trying to exchange contact information. Instead, I just told him to slide in my DMs. I was no longer interested in him. All he was good for was the money and that's it.

I put on my cover-up, said my goodbyes and bounced. By that time, I had sobered up enough to drive my ass home.

CHAPTER 6

hen I woke up, I had four text messages from Samir. He was checking on me and wondering why he hadn't heard from me. As much as I wanted to text him back, I didn't because I didn't want to lead him on. The 9-5 wasn't going to work for me, so I decided to block him. The man had bomb dick, but I was a high maintenance type of bitch and he couldn't fulfill those needs, especially not with a 9-5 job.

I checked to see if I had any messages from Siana and there were no messages from her. Slightly disappointed, I returned a few business text messages and emails.

I thought back to the pool party last night; my mind went to MoneyLongBoii. Who would've known that man was slanging a pencil dick? He flexed like his dick was long, but truth was, the only thing that was long was his money. Right at that moment, I remembered the money he gave me. I got out of my bed to look for my bag. I counted the money and it totaled eight thousand. *Not bad. After I deposit this money, I will use it to buy the Chanel bag I've had my eyes on.*

My mind drifted to Siana again. I thought about texting her, then I decided against it. I've been her best friend for years, and she had the nerve to diss me for a nigga. I wasn't feeling this new Siana, and I'm sure Zay is a dog nigga just like the rest of 'em. If Siana hadn't walked up when she did, I know he wouldn't have been able to resist all of this goodness. He tried to act all holy and back away from me, but I know that was all an act and deep down he wanted to see what it do.

If Siana wanted to act like a fool over me flirting a little, then so be it. She could kiss my ass, and Zay's bitch ass can too.

* * *

I CLEANED UP MY CONDO AND MADE SOME GARLIC MASHED potatoes, baked salmon, and steamed vegetables. As I ate my dinner, I read some of my DMs. Man, some of the messages I read were way out of line. Niggas were asking me to shit on their faces, some sent thousands of dick pictures. Some were asking to fuck, or suck on my toes. I ignored all of them. There was a DM from an influencer who was at the pool party.

She goes by the name StacksMami. She is not as popular as I am, but she is moving up fast. She's the color of dark chocolate with smooth skin and short curly hair, and her body is muthafuckin' stacked. StacksMami has big ass titties and the tiniest waist that I've ever seen on a woman, and her ass is plumped and shaped like an apple.

I opened the message and read it. She's inviting me to a spa party that is happening tonight. I'd never been to a spa party, but anything involving a spa sounded like music to my ears, and I was all for it. I sent her a message back telling her to send me the info. She quickly responded and told me to make sure that I dress in comfortable clothes.

I had to work on some sponsor posts for the Galores, then my schedule would be clear for the day. I relaxed a little bit and caught up on the show, *Love after Lockup*. It was getting so good I lost track of time. I quickly went into my walk-in closet to find something to wear to the spa party. I'm going to wear a white backless maxi dress and white sandals. I wanted to wear something that I could easily slide in and out of since I would be getting a massage.

The spa location was about fifteen minutes away from my place, so that was perfect. StacksMami told me that she rented out a place and had hired her own spa crew to give us massages, facials, and more. I needed this, so I was ready. I thought about bringing Joe or Keith, but I decided not to because it would be a chill night.

I MADE IT TO MY DESTINATION AND I IMMEDIATELY PARKED and entered the facility. There was a woman at the door checking names for this invite-only event. Once I was allowed in, I was led into a locker room and assigned a locker. I was also given a gift bag. Inside the bag was a soft pink robe, fluffy pink slippers, pink hair bands, and other little knickknacks. It was super cute and thoughtful.

I changed into the robe and made my way down a dimly lit hall to where the rest of the group was located. As soon as I entered, I stopped in my tracks. There was a large Jacuzzi in the middle of the room and four rooms surrounding the Jacuzzi. One room was for massages; the second room was for facials. There was a sauna in the third room, and the fourth room was an ice-cold sauna. I noticed twenty-five women were scattered around the rooms, and they were all naked.

I looked around for StacksMami and when I couldn't find her, I checked each room. I had one last room to check, and that was the sauna. I entered the dimmed room and I spotted her in a corner, spread eagle, eyes closed, head tilted back, and another woman between her legs, eating her pussy. I didn't want to interrupt, so I stood there watching the show. She still hadn't opened her eyes and it had been five minutes since I entered the room.

I wasn't into the female-on-female thing, but the way StacksMami was shaking and moaning, I wanted a piece of the action. I finally let my presence be known by tapping on her shoulder. She slowly opened her eyes and lifted her head. She smiled when her eyes landed on me. The girl between her legs didn't stop eating her out. StacksMami didn't even say anything, she held out her hand and waited until I placed my hand in hers. When I stood in front of her she untied my robe with one hand. Once I was butt ass naked, she guided my pussy right over her mouth. I didn't stop her. I gently sat on her face, and she hungrily sucked on my clit. She was moaning while she ate my pussy. I turned around to look at the girl who was between her legs, and she still hadn't stopped feasting on StacksMami.

I didn't stop riding her tongue, and she continued licking and sucking. "Yes, Mami… Suck this pussy…"

I was feeling the fuck out of this, but I was not ready to cum. We all were sweating like crazy, and I was surprised that none of us had passed out from the heat.

The door opened and in walked four more women. This is too much pussy in one room for me, but I wasn't about to crash their party. I was enjoying StacksMami's tongue between my legs. She didn't stop when these other bitches came into the room, so I didn't stop riding her pretty little mouth.

The other ladies must have been used to this type of event because one strolled right over to me and started sucking on my titties. Another girl went behind the girl who was still eating StacksMami's pussy and started eating her ass. The other two got into the 69 position and started eating out each other right in front of me. I'd done some pretty wild shit before, but never an orgy with all bitches. I went with the flow, but I was not about to eat any pussy. This session in the sauna lasted for another twenty minutes. I was on the verge of cumming when StacksMami suddenly stopped. I almost asked her what the fuck was she doing, but I held my composure.

"Let's take this into the main room where the Jacuzzi tub is at." StacksMami was smiling with my juices all over her mouth. She didn't even bother wiping it off. Instead, she winked at me and led the way toward the Jacuzzi tub as we all followed.

We walked into a real-life, lesbian fuck session. All the women had migrated into the main room and everybody was licking and sucking all over each other. I had never seen anything like it and my eyes were roaming all over the place. All I could hear was moaning, licking, sucking, and slurping sounds. I think the sound was turning me on more than the actual sex, but I'll be damn if I didn't get my freak on too.

"Come here, let me continue eating that juicy ass pussy of yours, Keiko."

StacksMami grabbed me before I even got the chance to respond. She got down on her knees to spread my pussy lips and went straight to work on my clit again. I looked around the room to see these bitches eating the fuck out of each other's pussies. My eyes landed on one chick in particular, she had the longest tongue I have ever seen. She was sticking it out while she played with her pussy, and her eyes were right on me. She slowly got up and came my way when we made eye contact.

StacksMami was still doing her thing and it was feeling so good, I checked to see where Ms. Long Tongue was at and just that fast, she was out of my sight. I did not know where she went that fast, but the next thing I knew, someone grabbed my ass. I turned around quickly, and there she was, Ms. Long Tongue up close and personal.

"The beautiful Keiko Kei. I've been having my eyes on you for a while."

This bitch knew who I was, however, I didn't recognize her from social media but I wanted to know who she was.

"What's your name?" I slightly turned my head to the side, and she leaned in close to my ear and whispered.

"PussySlasher."

Well damn, I didn't have a response for that. I had never heard of her, so I assumed that she wasn't as popular on social media, or maybe she was just a fan. She was actually very pretty. PussySlasher was light-skinned, seemed to be about 5'9, and curvy as hell.

She rubbed on my back slowly, then her hands slid down to my ass. She caressed my ass with both of her hands, then she spread my butt cheeks open. Seconds later, I felt that long ass tongue licking my bootyhole. She stuck her tongue so deep into my asshole, and for a minute, I thought it was a little dick. StacksMami was still eating me like I was the last meal on earth.

A petite woman walked over to us and put my hard

nipple into her mouth. I had three females pleasing different parts of my body. PussySlasher was going to town in my ass; StacksMami was sucking my clit like she was sucking a dick, and this petite, brown-skinned lady was flicking her tongue on my nipples. The muthafuckin' sensations were out of this world, and I wasn't going to stop them. My explosion was near as my legs weakened. Stacks-Mami must've felt it coming too because her tongue went straight to my vagina hole and waited for my sweet honey. I came so hard as PussySlasher and StacksMami held my weak ass up. I came all over StacksMami's tongue, and she caught every drop.

I sat down trying to recuperate because these bitches did some shit to my body. When I was back to normal, I went straight to the massage room. The ladies were still humping on each other, but I was done. I was ready to get my massage and dip. I looked back and StacksMami was busting the splits on PussySlasher's face. I thought about going back over there and getting another tongue lashing from one of them, but I was in dire need of a massage.

I walked into the massage room and I was happy to see that no one was on the bed. The masseuse was a young mixed girl. *I hope she was good with her hands.* My body was crying for a bomb massage.

"Hi, do you want a full body massage, or is there a particular area you would like me to focus on?"

The soft toned masseuse gave me my options. I chose the full body massage. I positioned myself on my stomach until I was comfortable. After I was settled, she started massaging my body. For such a small chick, she had strong hands and she did her job well, I was slowly dozing off until I felt a finger slide in my pussy.

"What the fuck!" I hopped up, forgetting the environment I was in.

Once I realized I was at the *spa party*, I got back on the bed. *Damn, everybody up in this bitch are freaks.*

"I'm so sorry, Miss. I was told that doing this is part of my job description for the night." The masseuse looked so scared.

"It's okay, I was just caught off guard. I do have one question though. Do you wash and sanitize your hands after every client?"

I was dead-ass serious. I didn't want no one's dirty ass pussy juice going inside of my pussy.

She laughed. "Of course, ma'am, but you are actually my first client tonight."

"Even better."

I got comfortable again and let this woman finish her duties. Her fingers found their way to my pussy hole again and slid back inside. I didn't think it was possible, but she massaged every inch of my hole. Her little fingers massaged it all around, in and out, and did some tricks that had my pussy pulsating.

Just that fast, I was cumming again tonight. My pussy sounded like mac-n-cheese as she continued moving her fingers around in my pussy and my juices coated her two fingers.

"Are you okay, ma'am?" she innocently asked me as she leaned forward to hear my response.

"I'm great. Thanks so much, you did a great job."

We smiled at each other, and I exited the room. I don't know what the fuck I got myself into tonight, but I had my first lesbian orgy. Now, it was time to bounce. After all of this, I was feenin' for a long hard dick.

I wanted to tell my gracious host bye. I looked around

until I spotted StacksMami standing in the Jacuzzi eating some woman sitting on the edge of the Jacuzzi with her legs open. I wasn't even about to disturb her. I left this pussy smelling room and walked my naked ass back to the locker room to get dressed. My night here was done.

CHAPTER 7

$\mathcal{I}$ woke up thinking about my life and how far I'd come. Yeah, I fucked my way to the top, but so what. I wasn't the first and won't be the last. I thought about last night, and my-oh-my, those bitches were wild as fuck. They had me cumming left and right. I had to laugh at myself. I was always getting myself into some shit.

My life was a fucking movie. I had everything I could ever ask for and more. I was what people considered an Insta-Baddie. I'm making money, making major moves, fucking whoever I want whenever I want, and partying with celebrities. Fuck, I am the celebrity.

* * *

Today, I need to take pictures for a company. Siana usually helped me with my simple photography needs, so I called her up. *I know this girl did not block me.* I stared at the phone as my call went to voicemail. I dialed her number again and it went straight to voicemail. I dialed her number one more time and once again, I heard her voicemail on the other end.

"Wow, this bitch."

I was in disbelief but fuck it. I didn't need Siana. My feelings were hurt, but I couldn't allow this shit to mess with my head. I will call Joe. He's been around long enough to know how I like my sponsor photos taken, and the extra pay for these extra services would be worth it. I called his number, and he answered on the second ring.

"Keiko, what's up with you?" Joe's deep voice resonated through the phone.

"Hey Joe, I need a huge favor. I know you aren't a photographer, but I really need your help with my sponsor pictures." I tried my best to make him hear how desperate I was.

"You know that I'm no photographer, but I will try my best," he laughed.

"Thank you so much, Joe. You can meet me at my condo in two hours, and I'll drive to the location where I want to shoot."

We ended the call. I was happy that Joe agreed to help me out. I went into my glam room to get the lingerie pieces that I needed to take pictures in. These pieces were very sexy and revealing. Two of the sets were crotchless for easy access. There were four lingerie sets total, and I wanted these photos to be different, instead of taking them inside my condo like I usually do, I wanted to be out in the open.

I was taking a risk by taking these pictures in public. Thankfully, I talked to a model a while ago who told me about a few places that were somewhat secluded or had no traffic at all. I was going to a hiking trail that overlooked the city. From what I remember, she said usually no one goes up that far. I was happy when she told me there is a road for us to drive all the way to the top. A bitch was not in the mood to hike for no damn pictures, so this was the best option for me.

I gathered all of the things that I needed, such as the lingerie sets, my heels, makeup, and my hair products. I didn't need too much; it will be a basic photoshoot using my cell phone. I would edit my pictures later using one of the many editing apps that were downloaded on my phone. I packed everything in my travel bag and got ready for my shoot. I turned on my Bluetooth speaker and Lil Kim's voice came blasting through the speaker.

"*I get paid just for laying in the shade, to take pictures with a glass of lemonade...*" Lil Kim said it best. This is my life. I continued singing the song as I stepped into the tub.

* * *

JOE AND I DROVE UP THE TRAIL AND THE VIEW WAS beautiful. As we drove, I was hoping that no one would come up here. *I'm not in the mood to explain why I'm on a hiking trail taking pictures in lingerie with this buff ass man as my photographer.* I giggled at the thought.

We found a good spot to park. I was glad that there were no other cars in sight. I looked around for spots where I wanted to take my photos, and when I found them, I got into my backseat to change into the first lingerie set. I was comfortable around Joe half-naked. He had seen it all.

"Alright Joe, we're going to the spot over there first." I pointed in the direction, which wasn't too far from my truck.

We were getting these photos knocked out fast and I was surprised to see that Joe was actually doing a good job.

I might have to hire him to take all of my sponsor pictures from now on.

"I have one more set to change into and then we can get out of here."

Joe nodded his head and stepped away from the truck so that I could change into my last outfit. We were wrapping things up, and I was happy that no one came while we were taking pictures. I threw my dress on and placed everything back into my travel bag. I looked around trying to locate Joe. I finally spotted him near a palm tree, taking a piss. He tried to turn at an angle where I couldn't see, but he couldn't hide that big ol' dick. I turned away because, as my help, I had never looked at Joe in that way before. Joe had to be about forty-five years old, six-foot-seven, dark-skinned, bald-head, full beard, and buff as hell. He never tried to come on to me, and it was always strictly business between us at all times.

I couldn't help myself, but I looked back over at Joe and felt my pussy throbbing. I don't know what came over me, but my legs started moving toward him. He heard me approaching and rushed to put his dick back into his pants.

"Please don't, Joe."

I reached for his dick, and it was even bigger up close. It had to be bigger than ten inches, and that muthafucka was thick, black, and full of veins. I needed to feel his dick, it was only right. I forgot about Joe being "the help".

"Keiko, let's go. We can't do this." Joe gave me a push toward my truck.

I know he is not dismissing me. "Please Joe, give it to me."

I could not believe I was begging for the dick. I was trippin', but I was not leaving until that big Black dick was busting my guts. He paused in contemplation and looked down at me.

"Keiko, I really don't want to do this because we have a really good business relationship."

"It's cool, Joe. We will continue to have a good business relationship."

I was determined to get Joe to fuck the shit out of me. I kept condoms in my truck, so I quickly went to grab one and handed it to him. There was no going back and forth with me, I was going to get what I wanted.

I grabbed his dick and stroked it until it was nice and hard for me. He was real nonchalant, but I know he wanted this pussy. When it got all the way hard, it could barely fit in my hands. *Oooh… he is going to rip my pussy walls.*

I opened the trunk so that I could lean into it while Joe fucked me doggy style. I opened my ass cheeks, making it easy for him to find my pussy hole with his monster dick.

"Mmhm, fuck!"

It felt like my pussy was slowly ripping apart as Joe's dick made its way to the inside of my pussy. My eyes rolled all the way to the back of my fucking head. I've had plenty of dicks in my lifetime, but his dick was by far the biggest I've ever had. I was enjoying every second of this pleasure and pain.

After my pussy was able to take every inch, Joe started to go ham on my shit. He had me creaming all over his dick. I must say *the help* was fucking the shit out of me. I was cumming back-to-back. He had me moaning like crazy. He had even started to make grunting noises. He was loving this wet ass pussy just as much as I was loving his monster ass dick.

I was throwing my ass back, and Joe was hitting it good. I still hadn't stopped creaming and it was all over the place. If I knew that Joe was packing like this, I would've been hopped on the dick a while ago.

Joe was fucking me faster and harder, so I knew he was about to cum. I threw my ass back even harder and used my hands to spread my ass cheeks wide open for him. I looked back at him, and he licked his thumb and it went straight into my asshole.

"Oh shit!" I shouted from the pain of his thick finger entering my butt.

He didn't stop, and I was good with it. After a minute that shit felt amazing. The pressure of his finger in my asshole and the pressure from his big dick drove me insane. I was on the verge of having an orgasm.

Joe gave me two slow long strokes before he stopped moving and let out loud grunting noises.

"Damn, girl," Joe said while he removed the condom and pulled up his pants.

I was stuck, barely able to move. I don't know what kind of dick Joe was packing; my whole insides felt shifted. After my legs stopped shaking, I pulled my dress back down and hopped into the driver seat of my truck. Joe got into the passenger seat and leaned the seat back.

The ride back to my condo was a quiet one. When we arrived at my parking structure, I looked over at Joe and my pussy jumped. He made sure I made it safely into my condo. I stopped him before he walked away.

"Thank you for helping me with my pictures."

I wanted to thank him for the bomb dick too, but instead, I gave him a smile.

"No problem, Keiko. You know I got you."

He closed my door and walked away.

CHAPTER 8

*I*n the morning I woke up to a sore pussy and ass. My body was feeling weak. All this sex all week had me beat. I wasn't going anywhere today. Memories of Joe clouded my mind. I wondered if things would ever go back to normal. I let my bodyguard hit, and that shit was great. *What the fuck did he do to my pussy?* I wanted more. I needed to snap out of it because this nigga works for me.

I slowly got out of my bed. I planned to lounge around my condo all day. I brushed my teeth and ran a bubble bath. I poured some Epsom salt into my bathwater and lit two peppermint candles. I turned on Summer Walker's album and eased my way into my large round bathtub. I was feeling relaxed and ready to fall asleep in the tub.

I soaked in the tub for an hour, and my body was feeling good. I changed into my loungewear and made myself lunch. I realized that I hadn't checked my phone all morning and that was a first for me. After noticing that my phone battery was dead, I placed it on the charger and continued making my lunch.

As soon as my phone powered back on, it was vibrating nonstop. I walked over to check why my phone was vibrating so damn much. I had thousands of notifications from my social media accounts, hundreds of text messages and missed calls. I did not know what was going on. I checked my messages first.

"What the fuck!" I shouted out loud. I could not believe what was on my screen. "How the fuck…" my mind was all over the place right now. Right in front of me, there was a picture of Joe dicking me down.

No way is this happening. Some people sent me the links where the photos were posted, and it was all over the gossip websites. I wanted to disappear. In bold, the title of the article is *Popular IG Model Caught Having Sex with Personal Bodyguard.*

How did we get caught? I thought no one was around. More so, how did they know it was me? As I continued looking at the photos, there were photos of my side profile, some of me looking back at Joe, and some of me holding my ass cheeks all the way open.

This cannot be happening right now. I got exposed fucking "my help". I was beyond embarrassed. Another article stated that I had sex with my bodyguard, who is a married man. I had no idea that Joe was married, matter of fact, we never talked about anything personal.

On social media, people were calling me an Insta THOT, a hoe, slut, and homewrecker. I was getting called every name in the book. People were tagging me in different articles. Someone even tagged his wife in my comment section. I clicked on her page to see who she was. She is around the same age as Joe, and her page was filled with many photos of their happy-looking family. Joe had two boys and seemed to live a regular life. I looked at a photo of his wife and thought about how lucky she is to be getting that dick consistently. The only thing that I was mad about was getting exposed.

People view me as this young perfect, rich, social media influencer who is all about looking beautiful, living glamorously, and getting money. Now I was being labeled as an Insta THOT, and even worse, I was caught fucking a man who had way less money than me. I needed to find out who did this shit.

I looked through my text messages again, and I saw a message from Joe. I clicked on it fast, and it read...

Keiko, I have really enjoyed being your bodyguard. However, we made a mistake and it will not happen again. I have to work on my marriage now, and by doing so I can no longer be your bodyguard. Thanks for everything. By the way, you can mail my last check to me. Thanks again. Goodbye.

Ain't this about a bitch! I was pissed, how can he just quit on me like this? Another text message popped up, and this time it was from my other bodyguard Keith.

Hi Keiko, I'm sorry about what happened to you and Joe. My wife has seen the articles and photos, and she no longer approves of me working for you anymore. I'm sorry, bye.

You gotta be fucking kidding me. Both of my bodyguards quit on me. I no longer have Siana, and now my bodyguards were gone too. The only three people that I trusted were out of my life. I was mad at the world. It was now my mission to find out who took the pictures of Joe and me.

I wanted to crawl in my bed and sleep for days, but I needed to keep myself busy. I checked my voicemails and emails. Everyone was talking about these fucking photos. I'd lost ten sponsors because of this mess. It was fucking with

my money. I was angry and seeing red. I turned off my
phone and threw it across the room. I was over this fucking
day.

CHAPTER 9

I was still fucked up about getting exposed. It'd been two days and I still hadn't turned on my phone. I've been in bed for both days straight. I showered, ate a snack, and went right back to bed. I had work to get done for the sponsors that were still rocking with me, but I just wasn't in the mood.

I turned on my phone and waited for it to load. Once again, the notifications flooded my screen. I turned it back off and got back into my bed. To make matters worse, I couldn't stop thinking about Joe's old man monster dick. The same reason that I was in this predicament now. Having an orgasm always eased my mind, so that's exactly what I was going to do. I pulled out my little pink vibrator sex toy and placed it right on my clit.

* * *

I MUSTERED UP ENOUGH ENERGY TO GET SOME WORK DONE, and now I did not have to worry about that for the rest of the day. Since I was up getting shit done, why not clean up my condo and finally face reality. I turned on Nipsey Hussle, and his voice surrounded my home through the built-in speakers that I had installed in my whole condo. Nipsey's music did something to my soul every time, it gave me all of the motivation that I needed. It was time to face this shit and say fuck what everybody had to say. People will always talk, and when the next big thing happens, this situation will be a distant memory.

I powered my phone back on and I didn't even bother reading the comments or anything that was related to Joe and myself. I cleared out my phone, blocked a few people on social media, ignored text messages from nosey ass people, responded to business emails, and I felt much better after. As soon as I was done, I heard my phone ring. I checked to see who was calling, and it was StacksMami.

"Keiko! Hey Boo! I've been trying to get in touch with you for two days. How are you holding up?"

She sounded energized. Flashbacks of her munching on my pussy popped up in my head.

"Hey Stacks, I'm holding up." I kept it real with her. I was holding up the best way I could.

"I'm not trying to get all up in your business, but don't even worry about that little bullshit. You gon' be good, and before you know it, people won't even remember this shit. Now, on to the two reasons why I'm calling you. One, I found out from a little birdie who took those pictures. Some nigga named Melo. I don't know if you know who he is, but I will send the link to his IG to you. Two, please, please, please come with me to the club tonight?"

StacksMami eagerly waited to hear what I had to say.

She had dropped a bomb on me. *That muthafuckin' Melo. I'm gonna get that nigga!* I didn't know how or when I would see him again, but it was going to happen one day. I couldn't let StacksMami know that I knew exactly who she was talking about. After going to her little "spa party", I wasn't quite sure about going to a club with her.

"Thank you so much, StacksMami. I will check out that link to see who this nigga is. About the club, I think I'm going to take a raincheck on that. Thanks for the invite though."

I needed to chill out for a minute. I probably should've taken her up on that offer so that I could get out of the house, but I didn't know what to expect with StacksMami.

"Come on, girl, you need a night of fun. I know you have been dealing with some shit lately."

She was starting to sound really convincing.

"Alright, you got me. I'll go. What time should I be ready?" I guess I did need to have some fun.

"Be ready at nine o'clock pm. I will pick you up if you want me to."

I could tell that StacksMami was smiling on the other end of the phone. I heard it in her voice.

"Coo, I'll be ready at nine o'clock pm, sharp. I'll shoot you my address."

I was starting to get excited about stepping out tonight. Going out always made me feel better. I walked into my closet to see what I wanted to wear to the festivities. I had so many damn clothes everywhere, I didn't know where to start. Most of my clothes still had tags on them. I picked out my short, orange, lace, body-con dress that I purchased a month ago from a cute online boutique, and my orange Christian Louboutin heels. I was stepping out in bad bitch mode tonight.

* * *

STACKSMAMI MADE IT TO MY CONDO AT EXACTLY NINE o'clock pm on the dot. I surprised myself; I beat my face, put on my blond lace front wig, and got dressed in an hour and a half. I was finished getting ready at 8:45.

I took the elevator down to the lobby. There were a few people in the lobby who immediately stopped talking when the elevator doors opened. *Perfect, this outfit has done its job.* I was looking good and smelling good. I wore no bra, and my orange thong was quite visible in this dress.

"Whoa! You look amazing Keiko! I might have to get a taste of that in the back of my car before we go into the club. Ha-ha," StacksMami laughed, but she was serious as a heart attack.

"Ha-ha. Girl, you are something else."

I was not about to feed into StacksMami's freaky ass. I was a freak, but this girl took the cake. She was on a whole different level.

"What is the name of the club we're going to?"

"We are going to Club Explosion."

She had a big smile on her face, so I instantly felt like I was about to get into some shit tonight.

"I have never heard of Club Explosion before, where is that?"

I'd never heard of Club Explosion, and I'd been to hundreds of clubs in Cali.

"It is in the valley, hun. Trust me, you'll have a blast."

StacksMami was hyped up. I was gonna take her word for it. I needed a night of fun badly, so I was going to relax and go with the flow.

"Girl, it's gon' be crackin' in the club tonight. Look at all those fine ass niggas and pretty ass bitches in line," StacksMami said excitedly as she stared at all the people in line waiting to get inside.

We drove around looking for parking and surprisingly, we found one near the club. At the door, StacksMami had to say a special word to the doorman for us to get in. *What kinda club is this?* I never had to do any secret shit to gain access into the club. She noticed my hesitant look and looked back at me.

"It's members-only, Keiko. Come on."

She grabbed my arm and led me inside. We walked right into a room that resembled a fancy walk-in closet. We had to leave our jackets, purses, and phones in this room. I was hesitant about leaving my purse and phone, but Stacks-Mami assured me that our belongings were going to be good.

Once we got inside the club, seeing that it was packed made me and StacksMami ecstatic. I don't know if it was the music, but I was ready to get on the dance floor. The DJ was playing my favorite female rapper, Lil' Kim, "How Many Licks." *This is my muthafuckin' song.*

I noticed right away this isn't an ordinary club. "Aye Stacks, what kinda club is this?"

I looked around and I saw all types of shit. There were BBWs, trans men and women, thug niggas, studs, gay men, midgets, men and women in business suits, and all different races in the building. It was definitely a sight to see, but this is a different type of mixture and I am here for it.

"Welcome to the best swingers club in town, bitch!" StacksMami shouted and started twerking on me.

"Wow! Girl, you should've warned me."

I was actually excited. Even though I heard of these types of clubs before, I had never been to one but always wanted to.

"I wanted to surprise you." She pulled me in and gave me the biggest hug.

"You are crazy."

I shook my head from side-to-side, and we both headed to the bar. I ordered us my favorite drink, Henny and pineapple juice. She wanted to show me around the place. This club was huge and there were fourteen rooms. There was a room available for every damn fetish or freaky shit you could possibly think of. There were rooms for people who love feet, dominatrix, trans, lesbians, gay men, people who loved getting pissed or shitted on, this room was locked up and in a shower type setting, fisting room, and there was even a room that had every damn drug that was ever made. I'd never seen anything like it. Each room was decorated to match the theme of the room, and they provided tools and items to help people make their sexual fantasies come true. I liked that each room had buckets of condoms. It was better to be safe than sorry in my opinion. However, not everyone was taking advantage of taking these safety precautions. In the biggest room, there were seats placed around a clear stage. I couldn't wait to see what would be happening on that stage.

"What is that stage for, Stacks?" My curious mind wanted to know what would be poppin' on that stage.

"That stage is for the grand finale that you will have to wait for at the end of the night."

She sounded anxious, so I assumed that whatever it was would be good. She continued showing me around the place, and right off bat, I knew where I wanted to start. The Romantic Love Room caught my attention. The room was beautiful. There were red lights, a red heart-shaped bed with candles surrounding it, a fountain with melted chocolate and fresh strawberries on a platter next to the bed and the floor was covered in red rose petals.

Of course, StacksMami wanted to go to the room

where all the lesbians were. *This bitch must not have gotten enough pussy at her spa party or something.* We agreed to part ways and do our own thing. While she was showing me around, I noticed a man who stood in the corner peeping out the scene, so approaching him would be my first move. He was going to be my first victim of the night.

"Why are you over here alone when there's so much pussy in the building?" I asked him seductively. He looked at me up and down with lust in his eyes.

"Actually, I was waiting for you. I noticed you when you first walked in, and I knew you would be coming my way," he said, cockily.

"Is that so? Well, I guess you were right. Enough talking, follow me."

I was ready to get my fuck on. He followed me right into the Romantic Love Room.

"This room is really nice," he said, admiring the room.

"Yes, it is. Take those clothes off."

I was ready to see what this six-foot-three, dark chocolate man was working with. I slid out of my dress and removed my heels. He kept his eyes on my body, and I watched his dick rise slowly. His dick was a decent size, but I wondered if he knew how to use it.

I looked at his naked body and I must say, Mr. Dark Chocolate was a sexy ass man. *I'm about to have fun with that chocolate bar, oh yes indeed.*

"Bring that ass to me now!" he demanded.

I did as I was told. He was sitting on the bed, dick sticking straight up and muscles poking out everywhere. I grabbed a condom out of the bucket and handed it to him. I watched him closely as he put the condom on. My pussy was on fire, and I was ready to feel his dick.

"Bend over."

He was taking control and I was feeling the fuck out of that. I bent my ass over, facedown, ass up. He went straight to work. This man was fucking me like his life depended on it. I was feeling so much pleasure from this rough sex. His chocolate dick went in and out of my wet pussy. The DJ changed the song to "Pu$$y" by Ty Dolla featuring Trey Songz. This song was perfect for the occasion because all of the attention was on my bomb ass pussy.

"You fuck this wet ass pussy so good!" This nigga had me moaning so loud.

"Good girl, you know how to take dick!" the dark chocolate stranger said.

The way he was talking to me was turning me on even more. I had my eyes closed enjoying the dick beating my pussy was receiving. When I finally opened my eyes, I noticed that we had a little crowd watching us. Since we had an audience, I was going to give them a show. No phones were allowed in the facility, so I didn't have to worry about muthafuckas taking pictures and making videos.

"Get on the bed," I told this stranger who was dicking me down.

He did as I said and looked at me waiting for my next move. I bust the splits on his dick and kept that position as I bounced up and down continuously.

"Oh shit!" his eyes rolled back.

I looked at our little audience and two of the guys were jacking off, and some of them were rubbing all over the women as they kept their eyes glued to us.

"I'm about... to... bust a nut!" Mr. Dark Chocolate said between moans.

I wasn't ready to cum yet, so I held back. I wasn't done fucking for the night, and I needed all of my energy. He laid on the bed breathing heavily, indicating it was time for me to move on to my next victim. I gave him a smile, grabbed my shit and gave his sexy ass one more look. A White girl crawled on the bed next to him and massaged his dick. This man wasn't even out of my pussy for two minutes yet and the bitch was ready to feel the pleasure that I was just getting. I don't blame her though. I was walking out of the room, but I stopped right in my tracks when I saw the White girl sucking his dick. I was disgusted. The condom that he used while he was fucking me was still on his dick. This White bitch sucked all of my juices off of the condom. I shook my head and made my exit.

I didn't see StacksMami anywhere, so I assumed she was still between some woman's legs or vice versa. I went to the restroom to freshen up, then I was going back on my hunt again. My pussy was still hot and ready for some more action.

In the restroom, there was a beautiful brown-skinned trans washing her hands. At first glance, one would think that she was a hundred percent female, but there were still a few features that stood out. I did not want to be rude, but I kept staring at her beauty. She had a brown wig with blond highlights and wore a tight sparkly jumpsuit. Her makeup was on point, and my goodness her body was curvier than a muthafucka. She caught me staring, and I tried to look away quickly.

"Hi honey. Your body is to die for! I want my surgeon to make my body look just like yours!" the beautiful trans woman said.

"Thank you, I'm sorry for staring at you. You are beautiful."

I was embarrassed, but she was a baddie for sure.

"Don't worry about it, honey. I'm used to it. You are beautiful too." She dried her hands while staring at me.

"Thank you, enjoy the rest of your night."

I moved over to a section in the restroom that was away from everyone to give myself a hoe bath. I wanted my pussy to be fresh for the next nigga. I looked back at the trans woman, and she was minding her business fixing her wig.

After I finished handling my business, I walked out of the restroom. Right across the hall in the Cloud Nine Room, my eyes landed on my enemy. That nigga Melo was sitting on a fake cloud staring at a big booty woman who was stripping for a group of men. My anger was starting to build up quickly. This is my chance to get some major payback, but I didn't know how. A light bulb went off in my head, and I came up with the perfect plan. I walked back into the restroom and approached the beautiful woman.

"I'm so sorry to bother you again, but I could really use your help." I normally wouldn't do this, but I was desperate to get payback for the humiliation that Melo caused me.

"Sweetheart, you are beautiful and all, but I will not fuck no woman," she said.

I laughed at her comment. I definitely didn't want that. I couldn't even imagine her fucking me.

"Ha-ha, oh no! I do not want you to fuck me, but there is a man out there that I want you to have sex with. I will pay you anything that you want."

My heart was beating fast as she stood there thinking about it.

"Details please."

Her arms were crossed on her chest as she waited for me to tell her my plan. I broke it down to her and told her exactly what I wanted her to do. After I was done, she was all in.

"Okay, I'm all in. Money talks, baby."

The trans woman, Angel, sounded even more excited

about my plan than I was. Angel was going to come on to Melo, and once he fell for it, she was going to take him into one of the rooms that would allow me to get a sneak peek of what was taking place inside. I just needed to find a way to get my cell phone without anyone noticing. I agreed to meet Angel at the gas station after the club to give her $800 for her services. I was excited and ready to set this plan in motion. I rushed to the room that held our personal belongings. There was a young man who was in charge of keeping an eye on our items.

"Hi sir, I need a little favor," I said to the watchman flirtatiously.

"What can I help you with ma'am?" he asked, licking his lips.

"I need my phone for a few minutes, and I promise I'll bring it right back." I hoped he would say yes.

"Ma'am there are no phones allowed inside the club. I could lose my job if my boss finds out." The young man sounded scared shitless.

"I promise no one will find out and you will not lose your job. I will give you $200." I smiled at him.

He hesitated for a minute. "What else can you give me?"

I know this little nigga did not. I didn't have time to waste, so I looked around and then entered the room. I locked the door behind me and pushed his little ass down. I pulled out his dick and started jacking him off. Four minutes later, he was cumming inside of my hand and I was walking out with my phone.

I looked around for Angel and Melo, hoping that everything was going as planned and Melo hadn't found out that Angel is a trans woman. I was hoping that by the time I reached them, they would be getting it crackin', so that I could get what I needed and bring the phone back before I got caught. I finally found them in the All Black Everything room. I was able to get a good view and stand in a section unnoticed. There was enough lighting for me to take a few good pictures and record a short video.

Angel was looking out for me and noticed me right away and gave a quick wink. Melo was too busy sucking on her fake titties to notice me. I don't know how Angel kept Melo's hands away from her private area, but she sure was doing a helluva job keeping his hands above her waist.

Angel whispered something in Melo's ear, and he rushed over to the area where the bucket of condoms were and grabbed one. By the time he made it back over to Angel, she was bent over ass tooted in the air. Melo was grinning from ear to ear. He had no idea he was about to fuck a transgender woman. From my angle, I could see that Angel used one of her hands to pull her dick and balls up, so that it would be out of Melo's way.

Melo got on his knees behind Angel and his dick easily slipped right in her asshole. Angel was rotating her ass all over his dick, and he was loving that shit. Melo closed his eyes and was pounding Angel's ass. Angel looked my way and smiled. It was game time. Just like we discussed, Angel lowered her dick just enough for me to take a picture and record a quick video. After I was done, I looked at it to make sure I had a clear shot of this nigga. It was perfect, the photo and video showed Melo fucking a trans woman clear as day. I looked back at them one more time and felt pure satisfaction. Payback was a muthafucka.

I went back to the front of the club to sneak my phone back into my purse. Now that my work was done, it was time for me to get some more dick in me. Before I looked for my next fuck, I was going to see what StacksMami was up to. It took me five minutes to find her in the Gold Juice room, getting pissed on by some Indian pretty boy. She was rubbing his piss all over her titties, stomach, pussy, ass, and legs.

"Yuck…" I said to myself. *I know that this heffa better use one of those showers to wash that shit off before she drops me off at home.*

I was going to check on her, but as I could see, she was occupied. I kept it pushing and looked around to see who I wanted next. I walked into the Dominatrix room. This room had black and red leather everything. In the corner, there were different costumes and sex toys that catered to this fetish. Even better, everything was brand new with tags. I went straight to the rack to pick out an outfit. I chose the red and black leather thong bodysuit. There was a woman in the room wearing all black leather lingerie. That shit was sexy as shit. She had a White boy on his knees while she spanked him with a thick leather whip. I wanted some of the action, so I walked over to them.

"Go grab another whip off that rack over there."

She pointed at the rack that had all of the whips that were neatly hung up. I grabbed the whip that matched my red and black leather bodysuit. I followed her lead, and whenever she brought down the whip on his ass, I did the same thing.

"I've been a very bad boy…" the White boy said in a whining voice.

Wham! Wham!

Our leather whips landed accurately, leaving welts all over his pale ass. I was loving this shit; being in total control felt great.

The woman roughly flipped him over on his back. She slowly removed her leather lingerie and squatted over his face. Then she just dropped down covering his face with her fat pussy lips. She aggressively rode his face, suffocating him. I could no longer see his face, and for a second, I was scared that she was about to kill his ass. Finally, she lifted up a little bit and he was gasping for air. Seconds later she sat right back on his face again. Her hands were grabbing his hair and pulling his head deeper into her pussy. Even though he could barely breathe, and his face was red as fuck, the man was enjoying this shit.

I no longer wanted to interrupt their little fuck session, so I left. Plus, I was still feenin' for some dick. As soon as I exited the room, I heard a loud ringing noise. I looked around trying to figure out what the fuck was going on. Everyone was leaving the rooms and rushing to the area where the stage was at. I glanced around, and I almost pissed myself when I saw Melo across the room. Shit, I couldn't let him see me. I kept my eyes on him to make sure I stayed out of his sight. Instead of going to sit down near the stage, he made his way toward the exit, and I instantly breathed a sigh of relief.

This room was packed, and there were a few available seats left. I scanned the room to see if StacksMami was anywhere to be found. We locked eyes at the same time, and she waved her hand signaling for me to come over to where she sat. I pushed and squeezed through the crowd. When I made it there, she pointed at the empty seat next to her.

"Hey, Keiko! Are you enjoying yourself?"

She was happy to see me. I looked at her and gave her a quick sniff. If this bitch smelt like piss, I was going to leave her ass sitting here by herself. She was naked and looked clean. She smelled like she just took a shower, so I sat back and gave her my attention.

"I am definitely enjoying myself, girl. This shit is crazy, bitch!"

I was actually having a good time at this club. There was so much to see and do, and I still had a lot more to experience. I decided to leave out the part about Melo. Even though she was the one who told me about what he had done, I still didn't know StacksMami like that. I wasn't quite sure if I could trust her, so I kept my mouth shut.

"It's about to get even crazier, boo," she said, giving my hand a gentle squeeze.

"Are y'all ready to get this fucking party started?" I recognized the voice, and when I looked toward the stage, it was Angel looking stunning.

"That's Angel. She's the owner of this club. Isn't she beautiful, can you believe she was born a man?" Stacks-Mami whispered.

"Wow. Yes, she is beautiful," I said. *So, this beautiful trans was the owner of this freak shit.*

"Y'all know what time it is!" Angel shouted into the microphone.

In her hand, she had a bucket. I was intrigued and anxious to find out what would be happening next. Angel moved her hand around in the bucket and pulled out two random names.

"Can I get StacksMami and Lolo to the muthafuckin' stage!"

I looked at StacksMami, and she was already out of her seat making her way to the stage. She was smiling and high fiving people. I looked at the other woman Lolo, and she looked Puerto Rican. Lolo had long curly hair, thick thighs, and a fat booty. She slowly walked toward the stage and men and women were getting their feel on as she walked by them.

"Ooowee, these asses are fat!" Angel stared at Stacks-Mami and Lolo's butts and made them turn around for the audience.

Everyone went crazy in the audience, shouting, clapping, and whistling.

"Alright now, calm down, my lil' horn dogs. Here are the rules for this week. Each man in the building will get to pump these sweet pussies up here. Whoever can take the most dick in ten minutes will win $10,000."

Angel broke down the rules and all the men were going crazy.

Oh, hell naw! I know StacksMami is not about to let all these different dicks get up in her pussy right now. I was a freak, and always ready to fuck different niggas but this is some other type of shit. I looked at her and she was on stage jumping for joy. Lolo was smiling and clapping. These bitches are wild. StacksMami was on one side of the stage and Lolo was on the other side of the stage. Each side already had about fifty men lined up. Angel was placing buckets of condoms on both sides.

Once everything was all set up, Angel got back on the mic. "May the best pussy win!"

She started her timer and the ladies laid on their backs. One by one, each man in line entered both StacksMami and Lolo's pussies. They were getting fucked by big dicks, small dicks, skinny dicks, fat dicks, pretty dicks, ugly dicks, short dicks, long dicks, Black dicks, brown dicks, White dicks, pink dicks, pale dicks. I've never seen so many different types of dicks under one roof in my life. I sat there watching these bitches take dick like their lives depended on it. Some of the men weren't even using condoms, and that was just straight-up nasty.

I could tell that StacksMami was starting to look

uncomfortable. I don't even know what number dick she was on; I lost count after thirty. Lolo was taking that shit and enjoying it all. This was probably something that she did often. Ol' girl was poppin' her pussy for every dick that entered her hole. I mean damn, I love dick and getting fucked too, but this is just too much.

StacksMami banged her hand on the stage, tapping out. There was cum all over the stage, and Angel almost slipped in it when she walked to the center of the stage.

"All this fucking cum almost made a bitch fall. I need the clean-up crew up here right fucking now!" Angel looked around for the clean-up crew.

"The winner of the $10,000 is the gorgeous, Stacks-Mami! She took forty-eight dicks, and Lolo was right behind her with forty-four dicks. Give her a round of applause!" Angel tried to hand her the bag of money, but StacksMami was still laid out on the stage. Lolo, on the other hand, angrily stormed off the stage.

I could see something was wrong, so I rushed over to StacksMami to help her up. First, I grabbed the money out of Angel's hands and we locked eyes. I gave her a slight smile, and she did the same. The crowd dispersed as I assisted StacksMami. Her legs were still open, so I looked down at her pussy. It was swollen, red, and bleeding.

"We need to get out of here right now, Stacks. Come on, let me help you up."

Angel helped me lift her up. There was a large t-shirt on the floor near us, so I quickly snatched it up and put it on StacksMami.

I went to grab our things from the front, and as soon as I walked in, the young watchman was licking his lips. I rolled my eyes at him and told him that I needed to retrieve my things as well as StacksMami's belongings because we were leaving. He could tell that I was not playing any games, so he rushed to gather our things. I met with Angel and Stacks at the front entrance and we walked to Stack's car. We made her lay on the backseat, and before I hopped in the driver seat, I stopped to talk to Angel.

"Angel, I really want to thank you for that favor. You don't know how much you've helped me."

I was appreciative. I reached into my purse to get her money, and Angel stopped me.

"Keep your money, sweetheart. That was an easy favor, and the man gave my little brown hole a good beating. Now, go take care of your friend."

Angel laughed, gave me a hug, and walked back to the club. I got into the driver seat and looked at Stacks. She was knocked out. I know her body was sore from all that fucking, so I looked for the closest Walgreens. I was going to get her some Epsom salt and run her a nice warm bath. I didn't want to drive back to my condo, so I booked a hotel close to the area.

When we arrived in the room, I ran her bath water and poured some Epsom salt into it. I woke up StacksMami, and she barely opened her eyes.

"Get in the tub Stacks, you need to relax in this water for a little bit."

I took the t-shirt off of her and guided her into the tub. She was weak as she slowly eased in. She sat in the bathtub and laid her head back.

"Kee... I'm sorry. Thank you for helping me. I thought a bitch could take dick."

StacksMami tried to make light of the situation by turning it into a joke. I giggled a little, but I still think that she should not have participated in that competition.

"Stacks, you are something else, girl."

I helped wash her body and guided her back to the bed after her bath. As for myself, I took a long hot shower. When I was done, I pulled out the sofa bed and got comfortable. I grabbed my phone to look at the photos and video of Melo. I smiled thinking about getting his ass back. I drifted off to dreamland with a smile on my face.

CHAPTER 10

I swear my life gets crazier and crazier. As soon as I think I've seen and done it all, *boom!* I find myself in more shit even crazier than before.

I looked over at Stacks on the bed sleeping peacefully like she didn't just take forty-eight dicks in her vagina last night. I know her pussy was worn the fuck out and beat down.

I ordered room service for us. I was starving, and figured she would be hungry too. I couldn't wait to eat and head home. Our breakfast came quick; I munched on my French toast, turkey bacon, and fruit. I read and responded to my business emails. I still had a few sponsors left, but my money flow had been completely compromised. Next, I checked my social media accounts and just that fast, people weren't really talking about Joe and myself anymore. The newest hot topic was a popular female rapper getting caught eating a married politician's asshole. She was tossing the fuck out of his salad in the photos.

I was feeling good, and happy that all of that negative

attention wasn't on me anymore. I was ready to go home, so I woke up Stacks.

"Wake up, Stacks. Wake up, girl," I shook her slightly to wake her up.

"Uh huh, what's going on?" StacksMami jumped up and instantly moaned out in pain. "Ouch!" She squinched her face.

She wasn't in the best condition to drive me home, but she looked much better than she did last night. I decided to book another night for her and called a driver to pick me up.

"I'm about to go home, but I booked you another night so you can rest up for a little while longer. If you need anything call me. There's breakfast on the table if you're hungry."

I walked over to get the food and placed it on the bed in front of her.

"I appreciate you, Keiko. You didn't have to do any of this. Thank you." She picked up a piece of turkey bacon and slowly chewed on it.

"No problem at all."

I gave Stacks a hug and left the hotel looking trashy in my orange dress that I wore to the club last night with my hair looking a mess.

* * *

I WAS CHILLIN' IN MY BED, MINDING MY BUSINESS, WHEN I heard my phone ringing. I looked to see who was calling and it's a popular club promoter from Los Angeles. He is called the Lit Master because everything that he is involved in is always lit. He only calls when he wants me to host a big celebrity party. Money is calling, so this is a call that I am going to answer.

"Aye, if it ain't the Lit Master himself!" I shouted into the phone.

"Keiko muthafuckin' Kei… My favorite Insta-Baddie. Look, ma, I know this is last minute, but my boy is having a huge party tonight. There will be nothing but rappers, NBA players, and NFL players in attendance. I need you to host this event. All these niggas keep requesting you to be the host, so you know I had to hit up my girl. For your appearance, they are offering you $20,000," Lit Master said, anxiously waiting to hear what I was going to say.

If he knew me at all, he knew that my answer would be yes as long as money was involved. "You already fucking know I'm all in!" I said beaming.

Money and ballers in the same room, I was going to be in paradise.

"Cool, I'ma text you the info right now, ma," Lit Master said as he hung up the phone.

My outfit needed to be on point. My hot ass cannot stay in the damn house. As long as money is involved, I am going to drag my tired ass out of this condo to get it. Last night at that swingers club, I didn't get to finish getting my fuck on, but tonight, I'm about to find me a rich nigga to fuck on and milk his ass for some cash. First, I need to get some beauty sleep for the turnup happening tonight.

* * *

I STOOD IN FRONT OF MY MIRROR ADMIRING MYSELF FROM head to toe. My hair is in a half-up half-down hairstyle; my makeup is done to perfection, and my outfit is going to be the showstopper. I am about to have muthafuckas gawking at me all fucking night. Just the way I like it. I got this outfit custom-made a while ago, but I never got the chance to wear it.

I'm wearing a black diamond bikini bra top that accentuates my full perky titties, and the matching high-waisted pum pum shorts, also known as booty shorts. *I hope I don't fuck around and get a yeast infection wearing this shit.* I might as well should have worn a thong or no pants because my whole ass and pussy lips are exposed in the shorts. To top it off, I am wearing black diamond heels that has straps that goes all the way up to my knees. I am looking good, smelling good, and feeling good.

I hired a driver for the night. I will be drinking heavily and don't need those problems. This is a night that I would have Keith and Joe with me. I shook my head because I lost my bodyguards over some bullshit. Shit, if Joe was still working for me, I probably would have tried to jump his bones again because that man had a pussy killa dick. My pussy jumped just thinking about it. I had to get my mind off that real quick; if I didn't, I would have to pull out my big Black dildo and fuck myself before going to this party. However, I would save that for another time.

* * *

THE PARTY IS IN HOLLYWOOD HILLS AT A MANSION MADE OF glass. It is beautiful and there are decoration lights everywhere. As soon as I walked in, Lit Master swooped me up in a warm embrace.

"Keiko, thanks for coming through for a nigga. You look fine ass fuck, like always, ma." He stepped back to get a better look at me.

"Thanks Lit, this place is dope as fuck. Whose party is this?"

I was still taking in the beauty of the mansion.

"It's the rapper Sincere's surprise birthday party. His boys wanted the baddest bitch to host the party, and that is why you were highly requested." Lit Master was grinning like a little boy.

"Well, they made the right choice. I am the baddest bitch," I said, feeling myself.

The place was packed, and there were a lot of well-known celebrities in the building. *Tonight is going to be a good night; there are dollar signs everywhere.*

Lit Master was still smiling from ear to ear. "Let me take you to the VIP section. You'll be in the same section as Sincere."

I followed closely behind Lit Master to a section that overlooked the whole place. We were able to see everything that went on in the backyard and inside the house. The whole setup is nice, and I fit right in.

"Y'all already know this lovely lady, Keiko Kei." Lit Master introduced me to the men who hired me and a few others who were hanging around in the VIP section.

"Hey everybody."

I smiled and waved at everyone. Just like I imagined, men and women couldn't keep their eyes off of me. I approached the men who hired me to host the party and shook each of their hands. There were about four of them.

"Thanks for having me."

"We had to hire the best for our boy," the tallest one in the crew said.

"I feel it."

They were pumping up my already big head. Sincere is one of the biggest rappers in the game. His songs play on the radio all damn day; he's in every popular magazine, and his following on social media is huge. People are always talking about Sincere, and that includes me too. He is fine as fuck, and his swag is out of this world. Sincere stay drippin' in designer shit from what I noticed on his IG. I was excited as hell to meet him. I know he had women up the ass, but none of those bitches were me. According to the gossip blogs, he never kept the same woman around for too long. He changed women as much as he changed his drawers. These hoes probably weren't doing a good job fucking and sucking on this rich ass nigga. Word on the street is that Sincere is worth over 600 million dollars. That is what the fuck I need in my life, a fine ass, big baller, nigga. I didn't know a lot about Sincere, but I was sure hoping to change that.

"What do you want to drink?" the tall one asked me.

"I'll take straight Henny, please."

I was ready to start drinking. I needed something to make me feel good until the man of the house arrived. I wondered if he would be upset that his friends planned a whole surprise birthday party in his home while he was away. He must've really trusted his boys for them to have access to his mansion.

"Can I have your attention, please?! Sincere will be pulling up soon. Everybody make your way up to the front!" The DJ announced over the mic.

Everyone rushed to the front of the mansion like "The King" was arriving. Everybody was so damn excited. The groupies even found their way to the party, and they were the first ones running to the front. *Damn, Sincere is the man.*

Instead of going to the front like everyone else, I went to the DJ booth. Since I am the host for the night, I was about to get on the mic and give Sincere a special birthday speech as soon as I laid eyes on him. I told the DJ my plan, and he gladly handed me the mic.

"Surprise!" I heard everyone scream out.

Damn, they are loud as fuck. Thankfully, there weren't many houses close to this one. If there were, the neighbors would be highly upset.

Five minutes later I noticed people making their way back, so I assumed that Sincere wasn't too far behind. I made sure everything on my body looked good and ran my fingers through my hair to make sure every strand of hair was in place.

I almost dropped the fucking mic when Sincere hit the corner into the backyard. I saw all the ice around his neck before I noticed anything else. This man looked even better in person. His smooth caramel complexion, hazel eyes, and neatly cut fade had me ready to lose my muthafuckin' mind. This man had a sexy hood swag that had me ready to bow down in front of him and suck his dick. His presence commanded attention, and he walked like he had all the power in the world. Groupies were salivating. Niggas were wishing they were in his shoes. No one could take their eyes off of him, and I was mesmerized by this man. I almost forgot about my little speech.

"Happy birthday, Sincere! Y'all give it up to this man on his special day! Enjoy ya night and everybody turn the fuck up!" My voice blared through the speakers.

Sincere looked around trying to see who was on the mic. When his eyes landed on me at the DJ booth, our eyes locked, and he gave me a bright smile. This man was doing something to me in a matter of seconds. Sincere was walking toward me, but his guests made it impossible for him to reach me. People were approaching him from left, right, front, and back. In due time, we would meet face-to-face. For now, I am going to go back to the VIP section to wait for him to finish greeting all of his guests.

I was feeling the liquor and wanted to dance. People were standing around drinking or trying to look pretty. Fuck it, I was about to drink, dance, and look pretty. I walked over to the glass dance floor with my drink in my hand and started gyrating to the reggae music that the DJ was playing. I was getting this party started the right way. Other people slowly made their way to the dance floor, and before I knew it, there was a full dance floor. What can I say, I am the life of the party.

Someone grab my waist from behind, and I turned around with an attitude wanting to see who the fuck was grabbing me like that. I turned around and stopped in my tracks. It was Sincere.

"Keiko Kei, I finally get to see you up close and personal."

He was so close to me, any movement would've caused his lips to be on mine. I'd never been star struck before because I was always around celebrities, but this man had me melting on the inside.

"Well, if it isn't the star of the night."

I was blushing like a muthafucka. Sincere was still holding on to my waist and dancing.

"You are the only star I see tonight. My eyes have been on you since I walked in here," Sincere said in a low voice.

I could tell he was high. He was cool, calm, and collected. He had this smooth demeanor, and I was falling for it.

"You got game, huh?"

I smiled at him showing him all the damn teeth in my mouth. I turned back around, and grinded my ass all over his dick that was slowly getting hard against my ass.

The DJ was playing all the freaky '90s R&B sex songs, so you know I was feeling completely hot and bothered. Thank goodness, I 'm wearing the black diamond shorts. If I was wearing a lighter color, everyone would be able to see my pussy juices right in the middle of these shorts. Sincere was dancing like he was making love to me. It literally felt like we were the only two on the dance floor. This nigga had it all. He is wealthy as fuck, fine as fuck, hood, and he is hypnotizing me with his beautiful eyes, dance moves, and his words. Sincere is the real deal.

"I don't play games, beautiful. No need to, I get what I want," he jokingly said, but I believed every word.

I finally snapped out of my trance and when I looked around, all eyes were on us. The men were undressing my damn near naked body with their eyes. Most of the women were staring at me with envy, and others were rolling their eyes at me. I didn't even care what they had going on, I had the attention of the richest nigga at this party.

The groupies were starting to do the most to get his attention. Too bad for them, he wasn't paying them no mind at all. His focus stayed on me. I needed to pee, so I excused myself.

"Hurry back, sexy. I'll be in the VIP section when you return."

He let go of my waist and watched me walk away. On my way to the restroom, I heard females whispering as I walked by.

"Ain't that the same hoe that got exposed fucking her bodyguard? Now she is all up on Sincere. Hoe ass bitch."

I almost went over there and punched the raccoon looking bitch in her mouth, but I had to check myself. I didn't want to be the cause of ruining Sincere's party, so I kept it pushing. That reminded me, this is the perfect time to leak those photos and video of Melo fucking Angel.

I locked myself inside the marble bathroom and pulled my phone out. Melo was a flashy nigga, so he had a few thousand followers on the Gram. People thought his poor ass was rich, but they had no idea he was fake rich. I created a fake email and sent an anonymous message to all of the popular gossip websites. I linked Melo's IG, along with the photos of Angel holding her dick while Melo fucked her doggy style. Satisfied with my email, I pressed send. *Yup, this nigga fucked with the wrong bitch.* I put my phone back in my black Balenciaga handbag and used the restroom.

Back in the VIP section, Sincere was laughing and smoking with his boys. His eyes were low, and I couldn't help but notice how good he looked sitting there in his zone. Just that fast I was feeling Sincere, and I wanted him.

"There goes my birthday host... Keiko Kei. Damn girl, you one sexy ass woman." Sincere passed the blunt to his homeboy and pulled me next to him.

"And you are one fine ass man."

I wasn't about to hold back or play hard to get. I was about to let him know that I wanted him. I don't give a fuck about any of those other bitches he had hanging around.

Sincere walked me back over to the dance floor, and we danced to one of his hit songs that was a banger right now. I twerked all over his ass while he rapped the lyrics to his song. I felt like we were filming for his music video, and I was having the time of my life. I ignored all the haters, and I gave him major props for giving me all of his undivided attention even though all of these people were here for him. We drank, laughed, and danced for the rest of the night.

CHAPTER 11

I had so much fun at Sincere's party. He even left his own party just to take me home in his custom, baby blue, Rolls Royce. I was going to invite him to come upstairs to fuck his brains out, but I decided to save that for another day. We exchanged numbers, and he promised that we would hang out soon.

As much as I wanted to lounge around my place, I have a lot of work to do. I need to film promo videos and this evening, I have to do a shoot for Crystals Galore. I am happy that I do not have to do my makeup or hair; it would get done professionally.

I sent StacksMami a text message checking on her, and she responded right away saying that she was good and thanked me again for everything. Now, it was time to check if Melo had been exposed.

As soon as I logged onto IG, many screenshots were being passed around of various articles with Melo's name and photos plastered all over them. *Perfect!* I bet this nigga is somewhere shitting in his drawers. I searched for his IG to see if he had posted anything, and it showed that his page was gone. *Yup, payback is a bitch.* That nigga is going to go into hiding forever, there is no comeback for a straight nigga getting caught fucking a transgender woman.

* * *

THE GALORES CAME GLIDING INTO THE ROOM WHERE I WAS getting my hair and makeup done. They walked over to me looking like they were dripping in money.

"Keiko, you are looking fabulous, honey. We brought the outfits, and they are waiting for you over on the gold rack. Usually, we do not come to the photoshoots, but we wanted to personally bring you the items ourselves," Mrs. Galore said as she held onto my hands.

Mr. Galore stood right next to her nodding his head while looking at my legs glistening with oil peeking out through my gold robe. *Yeah, I bet.* These freaks wanted to see my sexy ass again after that night of fucking. Both were fighting back the look of lust I saw in their eyes as soon as they walked into this room.

"I really appreciate the kind gesture. I'm sure you could have had someone bring the clothes here, but you two coming yourselves means a lot to me."

I had to fake it. I could care less if they came or not as long as I was getting paid. This is all business for me.

"Pardon me. Rachel and Cory, may we please speak to Keiko alone?" Mrs. Galore asked the makeup artist and hairstylist.

Oh lawd, what are these two up to now? I hoped they weren't about to try no shit up in here this evening. I didn't have time for it unless they were going to speak to me with some cash or a check in their hand.

Mr. Galore went to lock the door. They were up to something; now, I was curious. They came all the way to my photoshoot for a reason, and I was soon about to find out.

"Keiko, both my husband and I couldn't stop thinking about you after that night. I know you allowed my husband to have you, but now we would like to know if I can have you." Mrs. Galore looked at me with pleading eyes.

I didn't say anything at first, and as if Mr. Galore knew what I was thinking, he handed me a check. I looked down at the check and this time it was $100,000. My eyes opened wide, and I looked up at them.

"You sure can."

Money talks. I wasn't interested in getting my freak on with no old lady, but again, this is about to be easy-ass money and I was going to be $100,000 richer.

I was already naked underneath my robe, so I unfastened the belt on the robe and let it fall, exposing my glistening body. They stood there with their mouths hanging open. I noticed that she didn't remove her clothes, so I waited until she made the move. Mrs. Galore walked over to me and gently rubbed her small soft hands over my body. Mr. Galore leaned on the wall with his pink dick already in his hand masturbating.

Mrs. Galore turned me around so that my back was facing her. "Keiko, bend over and lean on the chair, please."

I did what she told me to do, and it wasn't long before I felt a wet tongue circling my bootyhole. These folks must have a thing for Black women; between her and her husband, I don't know who loved it more. She went to town eating my ass. We were all quiet, unsure of who was on the other side of the door listening. The only thing I was able to hear was Mr. Galore beating his meat and Mrs. Galore tongue licking me. This old White bitch knew how to eat ass. I backed my ass up a little into her face and that made her put her whole face in it. She didn't lick my pussy, she kept her focus on my dark tunnel. I wasn't going to cum from this, but I was going to let Mrs. Galore continue to get her rocks off. Mr. Galore's hand was moving faster and faster. It was almost time for him to bust. Just like I thought, I looked at him and his cum was shooting out in short bursts.

He walked over to where we were and picked up the gold robe that I was wearing and wiped the cum off of his hand and dick. *This muthafucka.* I shot him a dirty look.

"I'm sorry Keiko, I do not see anything else in here that I can use," he said in a low tone.

Mrs. Galore stopped eating my ass and cleaned her mouth off with the same robe. I shook my head. I had to put that filthy-ass robe back on.

"Thank you, Keiko. We'll wait in the next room for you. We'll stay for another twenty minutes to watch the first shoot, then we'll be on our way."

Of course, Mrs. Galore did what she did best and went right back to business mode. They unlocked the door and closed it behind them. I rushed to throw on the cum filled robe before the makeup artist and hairstylist entered the room. Mr. Galore's cum stuck to my back, and I was disgusted. In walked the glam crew, looking around suspiciously.

"Girl, we thought they were never coming out. Is everything okay?" Cory the hairstylist said.

"Yes, yes they wanted to discuss a business proposal with me. That's all. Um, where is the restroom?" I asked. I wanted to clean my now dirty back and wash Mr. Galore's cum off of my robe.

"Walk down the hall and it will be to your right," Rachel said while looking at me inquisitively.

I rushed off in the direction of the restroom. I still felt Mrs. Galore's saliva between my cheeks as I walked into the restroom. I quickly locked the door and removed my robe. I placed the area where his cum was under the running water and washed it off. This is so damn nasty, his thick white clumpy semen looked disgusting. Once I finished, I hung it on the rack while I cleaned off my back with soap and water. Then I washed my ass with water since there wasn't a bottle of body wash available. After I was all nice and clean, I went back to get my makeup and hair done.

I can't even front, the Galores new collection was bangin'. The bodysuits and two-piece matching sets fit me like a glove. I felt like a Queen as I posed in each piece. I was killin' this shoot and everyone in the room kept "oohing and ahhing". The photographer told me that the photos were going in magazines and one photo was even going to be on a billboard. Feeling happy was an understatement, I was beyond happy. I was ecstatic about that $100,000 check sitting in my purse. I could see that the Galores were satisfied with what they were seeing as well as they left the building with smiles on their faces.

* * *

I WAS EXHAUSTED AFTER MY PHOTOSHOOT AND FROM dancing all night at Sincere's party. *Hmm, Sincere, that man is everything that I need. Shit, Siana thinks she found her prince charming, Sincere is about to be my prince charming.* I could tell he was feeling me just as much as I was feeling him. I know he has a busy schedule, and so do I, but I can't wait to be next to him again. I wanted to call and tell Siana all about Sincere.

I pressed the call button and I heard Siana's voicemail. Pissed off, I called back again and the same thing happened. This bitch really blocked me. I was furious, but that was going to be the last time I called her trifling ass. I walked into my kitchen and poured myself a shot of Henny.

I listened to Kehlani while scrolling through my social media. Once again, my social media notifications were going up and text messages were coming through back-to-back. I clicked so fast as my heart pounded, *what the fuck now.*

I stared at photos of Sincere and me on the dance floor at his party. The article was titled, *Rap Star Sincere and Popular Social Media Influencer Keiko Kei, The New "It" Couple?*

Damn, these people are on it. We weren't a couple yet, but I sure hoped we would be. Now, this is the type of publicity that I want and don't mind. Everybody in my text messages were praising the photos of Sincere and me. I didn't bother responding to anyone. Instead, I posted a picture of myself in my black diamond outfit that I took at Sincere's party, and I had thousands of likes in a matter of seconds. I placed my phone on my nightstand and took my ass to sleep.

* * *

MY CELL PHONE BUZZED ON MY BED NONSTOP, WHICH WOKE me up. I looked to see who was calling and it was StacksMami.

"Bitch! You didn't tell me you were rocking with that fine ass nigga, Sincere!" she yelled into the phone.

"Girl, you gotta stop believing everything you read," I laughed into the phone.

"You could've fooled me because these pictures I'm looking at tells me otherwise. Oh, and by the way, did you see the photos that are circulating around with Melo and Angel? I didn't even know Melo was in the same club as us, did you?"

"I had no idea he was in the club. If I would've known, I probably would have beat his ass. Besides, I was too busy getting my fuck on to notice who was there," I lied.

"Well, somebody got his ass. Anyways, Mrs. Sincere, you got the world talking about you and Sincere. You are so lucky. I would do anything to get a piece of that." Stacks was starting to sound like a groupie.

"You need to be worried about healing," I laughed.

"Yeah, you're right. Can you believe that I'm still sore? I shouldn't even be thinking about sex right now." Stacks said sadly.

"You should probably take a break from sex, and just get yourself right because that was a bit too much for one person. Well, I'm about to go handle some things. Enjoy ya day, girl," I told Stacks.

"Bye girl, you too… oh and Keiko, snatch up that nigga Sincere," Stacks jokingly said.

I laughed at her craziness and hung up the phone. I looked through my social media comments and DMs and people were going crazy over the photos of Sincere and me. People were either rooting for us, talking shit, or envious. The crazy thing is we haven't even hung out yet. Muthafuckas on the internet are wild.

Just as I was placing my phone on the charger, my phone buzzed. I began smiling hard when Sincere's name popped up. I tapped on his message quickly.

Sincere: *So, I heard we are a couple now. *smile emoji**

Me: *I heard the same thing… LOL*

Sincere: *What are we going to do about that?*

Me: *You tell me…*

Sincere: *Are you free tomorrow?*

Me: *Yes, I am.*

I was still smiling, heart pounding against my chest, and feeling like that bitch.

Sincere: *A'ight cool, I'll come pick you up around noon, ma.*

Me: *OK, I'll be ready. *wink emoji**

Sincere: *Have a great day "girlfriend." Ha-ha*

Me: *You too… "boyfriend."*

I was elated. *This is really happening.* I fucked around with plenty of baller niggas, but Sincere have more money than all of those niggas put together. I fucked many niggas for the money, but I never really liked them… it was really all about what they could do for me.

Sincere is famous, filthy rich, so fucking fine, funny, and now, I just have to find out if the dick is good too. He is looking like the total package right now. Tomorrow couldn't come fast enough.

* * *

I GOT UP EARLY TO PREPARE FOR MY DAY WITH SINCERE. I planned to run errands and make sure all my stuff was situated before I left. My first stop is the bank to deposit the check from Mr. and Mrs. Galore. They were truly blessing my pockets big time, and I am not complaining. The shit was weird, but hey, *it is what it is.*

I was pressed for time, but I got everything done just in time to get ready before Sincere arrived. It was a little chilly outside, so I pulled out a burgundy two-piece legging set. It was a tight long sleeve crop top and matching leggings. I put on my burgundy and white J's. My hair was in a slick, sleek ponytail. I put on some fake eyelashes and coated my lips with Fenty clear lip gloss. I was keeping it simple and cute. I never had to try too hard, I have the type of body that looks good in any and everything and the face to match.

Twelve o'clock came, and Sincere was calling to let me know that he was outside waiting for me. I grabbed my Yves Saint Laurent burgundy shoulder bag and took the elevator down to meet him.

When I walked out, Sincere was standing outside leaning on his all-white Range Rover. He stood there looking all good and shit, wearing all white everything.

"You make a nigga wanna wife you," Sincere said as he held the door open for me.

I stepped into the truck and waited for him to hop into the driver's side.

"Wife me up then," I said to him as soon as his ass touched the seat.

"Maybe I will. We gotta see how you act first," he playfully said.

We both laughed and started our day. I had no idea where we were going, and honestly, I didn't even care. He had '90s Hip Hop blaring through his speakers, and he rapped the lyrics to each song that played. I didn't mind because I love anything from the '90s and knew some of the lyrics too. I wasn't a rapper, but I rapped the lyrics right along with him. We were having so much fun that I didn't even notice that he was still driving and on his way to San Diego.

He lowered the volume, "I hope you don't mind, ma, but I want to get away for a lil' bit. I have a condo in San

Diego that I never go to, and I thought that this would be the perfect time."

"I don't mind at all, I'm just here for the ride."

He smiled at me and held my hand. For the rest of the ride, we were holding hands. Just that quick this man was making me feel good.

We arrived in San Diego and pulled up to a parking structure that belonged to the residents who lived in the luxury condos. My condo is beautiful, but the way these condos looked from the outside, I knew that the insides had to be even better. Sincere parked, and hand in hand, we walked to a side door. I wondered why he didn't enter the main lobby, but I was going to find out soon. He used his key to open the door and we walked into a room that only had an elevator. Once we were inside the elevator, he pressed the only button that was available. The elevator went up for a while before it opened up to a beautiful view of the ocean. I was absolutely amazed.

"This is beautiful!" I walked over to the floor to ceiling windows that surrounded the room.

"Thank you, but the only thing beautiful is you," Sincere said as his eyes pierced my soul.

He was making me feel a way, and if he was anyone else, I would be fucking the shit out of him right then and there. I held my composure, though. Our time would come. I turned around to face him, and he was already standing behind me. He got closer and our lips touched. His lips were extremely soft. We stood there tongue kissing while he massaged my ass with his big strong hands.

Two minutes later, our tongue kissing session ended. He stepped back and just stared me down.

"Come on, ma. Let's go inside." He guided me toward a door that I hadn't noticed before.

"Damn, there's more?" The view from this room was breathtaking, nothing more was needed.

He laughed. "Of course there's more, this room is only to separate my condo from the elevator. I own the whole top floor of this building. I'm the only one who has access to that side door we used to get up here. I like to slip in and out unnoticed, so to avoid stepping foot into the lobby, I have my own entrance."

"Oh, wow. So, you big time."

I played it off, but I was feeling him even more. I couldn't wait to see his actual condo. We walked in, and I almost passed out. I thought my condo was on some luxury shit. Sincere's condo was four times bigger than my condo and everything was black, white, and silver. It looked like he hired an interior decorator. Everything looked expensive, even the small pieces that he had placed around.

"Let me show you around."

He led the way and I followed closely behind him. There are a total of four bedrooms and four bathrooms, and each one looked like they could be master bedrooms and master bathrooms. I looked around imagining myself living there with him. He even had a gym in his condo. I felt like we were in a mini-mansion. We walked into his room, and his custom bed looked like it could fit eighty people. I didn't understand why he had such a big bed for only one person, but I guess when you have money, you can do anything and buy anything just because. Everything in his room was lavish. He had a huge painting of himself on a stage hanging on the wall above his bed.

"This is a nice painting, Sincere." I stood back admiring the painting.

"Thanks, luv. A fan in Paris painted it for me."

He looked at the painting for a minute then walked out

of the room. I followed right behind him. This place was huge. The floor to ceiling windows that surrounded the whole place made me feel like I was in my own world in the sky. I felt like I was on top of the world, and being with Sincere made things even better. This is the life that I deserved. Yeah, I had my own shit, but this is a different type of living, and I wanted it all.

"You good, ma?" Sincere held me from behind and placed small kisses on the back of my neck. I looked out the windows staring into the ocean. This view was everything.

"I'm good. I'm just admiring your place. I thought my condo was something special, but after seeing this I think differently now." We both laughed at the same time.

"This ain't nothing, just my getaway spot when I don't feel like being bothered." Sincere shrugged his shoulders.

"You hungry? I can order whatever you want and have it delivered. They will place it in the room where the elevator is located."

"Yes, I am, can we get some pasta?"

I was starving. He went into the kitchen drawer and pulled out a menu. Sincere handed me the menu and told me to choose whatever. Everything on the menu looked delicious, and we had a hard time selecting one dish each. Between the two of us, we ordered like six dishes. This is way too much food for two people, but it was okay; we would have leftovers for later.

* * *

I DIDN'T HAVE ANY CLOTHES TO CHANGE INTO, SO SINCERE told me not to worry. He pulled out some special high-tech tablet and passed it over to me. I didn't know why he was giving it to me until I looked at the screen.

"You can get whatever you want, luv. I don't like going out shopping because paparazzi stay on my ass, and I can never shop in peace, so I use this app wherever I go. You put in your location and there's a group of professionals who go and pick up whatever you order and bring it to you right away. It is members only, and I pay a lot for this service every year, but it's worth it."

He was so nonchalant. I sat there looking at him in admiration. Yeah, this nigga was rich-rich. There were so many high-end stores to choose from, I didn't know where to start. He did tell me to buy whatever I wanted, so I did just that. I picked out eight outfits, and eight pairs of shoes to match each outfit. After everything was in the cart, I wanted to be nosey and see how much everything totaled up to, even though he told me to hand him the tablet when I was done.

Oh shit, the total amounted to $50,000. I slowly handed the tablet to Sincere, waiting to see what he would say.

"That's all you want?"

He looked over at me like that wasn't shit. I thought about adding more items, but instead, I said, "Yes, that's it. Thank you."

He purchased my items, and I was happy as fuck to get some bomb ass outfits and shoes. I was ready to see what that dick do though. I was surprised he hadn't tried to have sex with me. I know he was used to getting pussy easily, so I played it cool for now.

We chilled and watched reruns of *Martin*. I learned that Sincere was an only child, and his parents were deceased. They died in a car accident when he was just a child. His grandmother raised him, and when he turned eighteen, his grandmother passed away from natural causes. Shortly after his grandmother's death, he got signed with one of the biggest record labels in Los Angeles. I thought Sincere was older, but he was only twenty-six years old. He knew a lot, but I guess that came with life experiences. Sincere and I had a lot in common. I was so happy that he didn't have any kids. I did not want to have to deal with no crazy baby mamas.

Sincere's phone vibrated, and he looked to see who was calling. He got up and went to the front door. He disappeared around the corner and came back with bags.

"Here are your clothes and shoes, ma." He placed all of the bags in front of me. I felt like a kid in a candy store.

"Thank you so much, Sincere!" I jumped up and pulled him in for a tight hug.

"Welcome luv, there's more where that came from."

He pulled me closer to his body. I couldn't hold it in anymore. I wanted him. I needed to feel him deep inside me. I started tugging at his belt buckle and unzipped his pants. He didn't stop me, so I continued. Sincere stepped out of his pants and Calvin Klein boxer briefs and removed my clothes in the process. Before I knew it, we were both butt ass naked. He pinched my hard nipples between his fingers and replaced his fingers with his mouth. *Ooooh, his dick looks so tasty.* It was nice, long, and thick. It was perfect. I couldn't be happier. In my eyes, he is the perfect package.

I jacked him off while he sucked on my nipples. My pussy got moist. I squirmed a little, anxious to feel him. Sincere stopped and swiftly walked away. I know this nigga was not leaving my horny ass hanging.

He came back as quickly as he left. He was holding a Magnum condom in his hand. Before he could get it open, I pushed him down on the couch and kneeled between his legs. I wanted to taste his dick, and I was not trying to taste no damn rubber.

"Damn, ma, like that?"

Sincere looked down at me between his legs with a smile on his face. I filled my mouth with his big dick. I went ham on it. I slurped, jerked, licked, sucked, and spit all over his dick and balls like I was competing for a dick sucking contest. There was no holding back. The tip of his dick was hitting the back of my throat, and I was gagging like crazy but that didn't stop me. It made me go even harder. Sincere had his head laid back and his right hand was guiding my head up and down on his dick.

"I'm bout' to cum, ma…" He barely got the words out of his mouth.

That was my cue to keep slobbing on his knob even harder. His warm cum filled my mouth and slid down the back of my throat. I swallowed every drop and licked my lips after I was done.

"Tasty," I said to him.

"Oh shit, you just sucked the soul out my dick."

He stared at me seductively. I knew what the fuck I was doing, and I did just that… sucked the soul out of his dick with no hesitation, and it was damn good too.

After a few minutes, he got up and flipped me over his shoulder and carried me to the kitchen counter. He aggressively kissed me on my lips, and I did the same thing back. We acted like two horny teenagers. Sincere leaned me back on the counter and popped my nipple in his mouth. He showed love to both nipples before he slowly licked downward leaving a wet trail on my stomach. When he reached my pussy, he pushed my legs back exposing my whole pussy and asshole. Sincere licked and sucked all over my pussy and asshole. Nothing was off-limits. He flicked the tip of his tongue back and forth, fast on my clit. That shit drove me wild. My toes curled and my eyes rolled back. I was shaking and cumming all over his kitchen counter. He tongue fucked my pussy and ass, causing me to have multiple orgasms. I don't know what the fuck he did to me, but a bitch was sprung that fast. He picked me up and carried me back to his plush couch and laid me down. He grabbed the condom off the coffee table and slid it on his dick.

"Put it in, daddy..." I didn't give no fucks at this point. I needed the dick.

Sincere's dick fit perfectly inside me.

"How this dick feel, ma?"

"It feels sooo... good... oooh... ahhh... Fuck... shit... damn..." I said between moans.

He was pounding my G-Spot and juices were pouring out of my vagina all over his dick and the couch. This nigga had that dope dick, and I was surely getting addicted to it. He flipped me over and pushed my head down with my ass up in the air and fucked me doggy style. When he wasn't slapping my ass, he was pulling my hair or choking me. I was loving this ghetto sex, and he was turning me out and turning me on.

"Yeah, that's right, take this dick." He was pumping even harder and faster than before.

"Fuck! Yes! Damn this dick is good, daddy! You fuck me so good!"

Everything was coming out of my mouth, and my pussy was hurting good. This is the type of dick that would make a bitch go crazy.

"This my pussy now Keiko, you betta not give this shit to nobody," Sincere said to me.

I don't know what it was, but hearing that shit made my pussy get even wetter.

"It's yours, daddy. It's yours..."

He could have all of me. He's paid and got good dick. Yup, he can have anything his heart desires.

For the rest of the night, we fucked in every damn room he had in his condo. Sincere went through the whole box of condoms, and I wasn't complaining at all. It was 5:00 am by the time we finished our last round. We were both hungry and worn out. I warmed up the leftovers, we ate, and then we were knocked out wrapped up in each other's arms. *Life is good.*

or the next two months, Sincere and I were inseparable. We did a good job trying to stay under the radar. He came to my condo sometimes, but I was mostly at his Hollywood Hills mansion. I called that mansion the glasshouse. I loved being with him. I thought that I knew a lot, but Sincere was teaching me things daily. Investing, ownership, history, and so many other things. I know it was fast, but I was starting to fall in love with him. We weren't even officially in a relationship, so I was not going to look stupid and tell him yet. I was spending a significant amount of time with Sincere and was getting whatever I wanted from him. He stayed giving me racks on racks. I didn't want for anything. Why spend my own money when I could spend his money. The icing on the cake was that he was dicking me down on a daily basis. What more could a girl ask for. I had it all. I even stopped fucking with different niggas, because I was getting everything that I needed and wanted, plus more from Sincere.

My contract with the Galores would be ending soon

and I was happy about that. I no longer wanted to do anything that would take time away from being with Sincere. Most of the sponsors that I had were also coming to an end and I didn't mind at all. I wasn't hurting for money. I would have more than enough time to give Sincere all of my attention whenever he wasn't in the studio, on tour, or handling his business.

* * *

"CONGRATULATIONS, YOU'RE PREGNANT."

I sat on the hospital bed frozen like a deer in headlights. *I can't be pregnant, no, no.*

"Dr. Snow... how far along am I?"

I could barely get the words out. *How did this happen?* I thought back and realized that I was so caught up in living life with Sincere, I hadn't had my period in a while.

"You're almost three months, Ms. Konners."

The doctor patted my back with a concerned look on her face. She could tell that I was not happy.

"Is everything okay?" Dr. Snow asked when the tears slowly ran down my cheeks.

"Uh, yes. Thanks. I have to go."

I grabbed my purse and rushed out of the doctor's office. I heard her call out my name, but I didn't look back. I kept going until I reached my truck.

"Why!" I continuously hit my steering wheel with my hands.

This couldn't be happening right now. If I was almost three months pregnant, that meant that the only person it could belong to is Samir. He was the only one I had unprotected sex with. Flashbacks of us having sex on the Ferris wheel ran through my mind. *Fuck, I need to get this handled quick.* I hadn't thought about Samir since I blocked him. *I can't have a baby right now. I definitely can't have a baby with a man who works a 9-5.* If Sincere was the father, it would for sure be a different story.

I couldn't let Sincere know about this. I looked down at my belly, and there was a small pudge that I hadn't noticed before. I was always careful, until that one time I slipped up, and now, here I am pregnant. *How did I not know that I'm pregnant?* Then it hit me, this is why I've been feeling so nauseous lately. I thought that it had something to do with the alcohol Sincere and I downed every day, but the whole time it was this pregnancy.

I went to the doctor to get my yearly pap smear and found out that I'm pregnant. I don't know how I made it home in a daze. Thank God Sincere would be busy working on his new album in New York because I needed to find somewhere to get an abortion ASAP. I was dealing with Sincere now, and I couldn't allow anything to come between what we have going on.

* * *

THE COLD GEL SMEARED ALL OVER MY BELLY WHILE THE nurse did an ultrasound to see my fetus. The screen was facing me, and I turned my head. I couldn't look at the little fetus that was growing in my womb. My heart thumped rapidly, and I couldn't shake the nervousness. One minute I was living it up with my bae, Sincere, and the next minute, I'm in this clinic on a bed preparing to get rid of another nigga's baby. I know it all happened before meeting Sincere, but I still felt guilty for doing this.

I was going to have a surgical abortion, and I was ready to get it over with. I felt even worse for what I was about to do when I walked by the protestors outside the clinic. I couldn't even make eye contact with any of them.

I didn't have anyone to drive me home after my procedure, so I hired a nurse to drive me home and help me for a few days. This is a time that I wished Siana and I were still cool. I needed her right now, but she still did not want to have anything to do with me. I missed her like crazy, but I was not about to fight for a friendship that she no longer wanted. I thought about contacting Samir to let him know what was going on, but I decided not to. There was no point in doing so.

The nurse explained the procedure to me and moved me into the surgical room. She informed me that when I woke up, I would be in a room with other women. That couldn't happen, because of who I am, so I had to pay extra for a private room. I didn't care about the cost. I was not going to risk being exposed for some shit like this.

They wheeled me into the surgical room, and soon after they put me to sleep. As my eyes closed, I asked God for forgiveness.

* * *

THE NURSE THAT I HIRED WAS THE BEST. SHE WAS AN OLDER Jamaican lady with an accent. She knew exactly what I had done and there was no judgment. Nurse Clarke made my breakfast, lunch, and dinner. I was feeling better two days after my procedure, but I asked her to stay with me for the week. I was finally starting to feel like myself again, and I enjoyed listening to Nurse Clarke's old stories from her childhood in Jamaica. She felt like the grandmother I never had. When it was time for her to leave, I didn't want her to go.

"Nurse Clarke," I held onto her arm and rested my head on her shoulder.

"Yah, sweetie?"

Nurse Clarke's accent made me smile every time. Sometimes I didn't understand what she was saying, but it was still comforting to hear her speak.

"I really appreciate all of your help this week. I don't think I could've made it without you here. I hate that this is your last day. If you don't mind, I would like for us to keep in touch," I sadly said to her.

"Of course, mi dear." Nurse Clarke patted the back of my hand. She got up to write down her number, email, and address for me on the notepad that I kept on my kitchen island.

"Thank you."

I gave Nurse Clarke a hug and gave her a small envelope that had a piece of paper with my contact information on it and a check. I was going to give her an additional five thousand dollar tip. She went above and beyond for me this week, and I was appreciative of it all.

Nurse Clarke thanked me, and she rolled her small carry-on bag out the front door. I waved her good-bye and closed the door behind her.

I went to my phone and noticed that I had two missed calls from Sincere. I was missing his ass like crazy. We briefly talked this week, and I was a little happy about it. I was healing from my abortion and it was a rough week for me mentally. I hurriedly pressed the call button.

He answered on the first ring. "Baby girl, I miss you. I need to see you soon. I'm wrapping up this album, and I'll be done in the next week or so. Then we'll be able to spend time together again."

His deep voice sounded so good on the phone. "I miss

you too, bae. I can't wait to see you again. I know your album is going to be amazing, I can't wait to listen to it," I said excitedly.

"Matter-of-fact, I'm going to fly you out here in a week. Be ready, ma."

"Okay, baby. I can't wait to see you!"

He let out a quick laugh and we ended the call. That was perfect. I hoped that I would be okay physically. He is going to beat my pussy up when I arrive in New York, so I have to get prepared for my bae. I probably shouldn't be thinking about getting dicked down so soon, but I couldn't help it. Sincere is that nigga, and he have my ass wide open and ready to risk it all for him.

Everything is falling right back into place. I wasn't pregnant anymore and I'm feeling good again. It was my last week with the Galores, and after I finished these last few sponsor posts, I will be free to do me. I was going to put a pause on booking jobs in the meantime. I needed a break from work and I wanted to be able to freely spend as much time with Sincere as I wanted to.

CHAPTER 13

a week flew by quickly. I was packing up my bags because a bitch was getting flewed out. Sincere texted and called me all week telling me that he couldn't wait to see me. We were on the same page because I couldn't wait either.

I packed outfits for every occasion. I had an outfit for lounging around, clubbin', chillin', swimming, casual attire, dressy clothes, and even outfits for a fuck fest. You name it, I had it, and if I didn't have it, Sincere wouldn't have a problem getting it for me.

I no longer had any obligations that would hinder my plans. All of my jobs were complete, and I was relieved. It was time for me to live it up with Sincere by my side. My flight was leaving at midnight, and I did not want to be late.

I wanted to look good for Sincere, so I booked a hair-stylist to come to my condo to install a 28-inch weave. I got my nails and toes done in the comfort of my home. The mani and pedi were exactly what I needed. My pussy and ass needed to be waxed too, so my wax lady came over. My

hair was laid, nails done, and my pussy and ass were hair-
less and smooth. I was back to normal, and it felt fuckin'
great.

* * *

I LANDED IN NEW YORK CITY. SINCERE HAD HIS PERSONAL
driver waiting for me at the airport. I had no idea where
the driver is taking me, but I sat back in the comfortable
seats and relaxed while admiring the tall buildings we drove
past. I had more than enough space in the black Cadillac
Escalade truck.

Forty minutes later, we pulled up to a black gate, and
the driver punched in a code to get in. He pulled in and we
drove by exotic cars. *Damn, I don't know where we are, but it
seems like everyone inside the gate has money. This is what the fuck
I'm talking about.*

The driver opened my door to let me out and escorted
me to another smaller black gate. He punched in another
code and a buzzer went off, which allowed us access into
the building. We walked into a room and the aroma of
weed hit me right in the nose. It was so smoky in the room,
I could barely see anything. From what I could see, there
was a red couch, a table with snacks and drinks, and every
drug that you can imagine laying right out in the open. A
few men and women were sitting and standing around
indulging in drugs, drinking, and eating snacks.

The driver continued walking toward another door, and
I was right on his heels. In the next room was a large studio.
This room was different compared to the other room. In
the studio, there was high-end music equipment, leather
black couches, and a few people scattered around. I looked
around to see if I could spot Sincere, and he was sitting at a

table looking through a notebook. He looked up when the door closed.

"Baby, you made it!"

He was so happy to see me. I ran into his arms, and he hugged me like he didn't want to let me go.

"I'm finally here, babe."

I stared into his eyes and our lips connected. Others in the room looked at us, said hello to me then exited the room to give us our privacy.

"I'm about to get in the booth soon, but first I need to feel you, ma, with yo beautiful self. You look so fuckin' good."

Sincere was so close to my face, I could smell the weed and alcohol on his breath.

"Right here?" There were so many people on the other side of the door.

"They won't bother us. I own this studio and pay everyone who is in this building. And, the studio is soundproof."

He is so cocky and I love it. He played some music, and I knew right away that it was one of his new songs. He was rapping about fucking in the studio.

I removed my heels, jeans, my crop top, and stood in front of him naked. He turned me around to get a good look at my body from every angle. I modeled my naked body and jiggled my ass a little bit for him.

"You got my dick rock hard, baby."

He pushed me down toward the floor on all fours and bent me over. I arched my back just the way he liked it and waited for him to slide his dick in my sweet hole. I heard him fumbling to open what sounded like a condom wrapper.

His hard dick slid right in, and I jumped from the mild

discomfort. I knew it had to be from the abortion only happening two weeks ago. I prayed that I didn't start bleeding. It didn't take long for my pussy to adjust to the feeling of having a big dick in it. I threw it back on him and he was beating my pussy the fuck up. Thankfully, the studio was soundproof. I was moaning and screaming out Sincere's name, curse words, and other sounds. The hood in him always came out when we fucked. That hood shit was such a turn on and kept me creaming all over his dick.

After we were completely satisfied, he kissed me softly on my lips. He threw the condom in a nearby trashcan and cleaned off his dick with the baby wipes that he had in a duffle bag that sat next to the couch. He handed me the pack of wipes, and I thoroughly wiped off my pussy, and wrapped it up in another clean wipe before discarding it. I put my clothes back on and took a seat on the couch. The air smelled like sex, and Sincere must've read my mind because he grabbed the ocean breeze air freshener that was on a table in the corner and sprayed the studio.

He texted someone, and in walked the whole crew who was in there when I first got here. Everyone acted normal and went back to doing their duties. Sincere walked into the booth and zoned out.

I sat on that couch amazed at the skills this man possessed. He had everybody in the room hypnotized. They were dancing, bopping, and nodding their heads to the music. It felt like we were at a live concert. Sincere is truly a star. I was falling harder for him. He was freestyling and going hard in that booth. He zoned out into another world when he is rapping.

"Dreams of fuckin' Keiko Kei on my private jet, legs spread, diggin' out her guts..." The music blared loudly into the speaker that surrounded us in the studio.

Wait, did I hear what I think I just heard? He said my name in his song! Oh my gosh! I was feelin' like the baddest bitch. Sincere had me on a natural high. This shit felt like a movie, and I was the star in it.

We left the studio four hours later, and I was drunk and tired, but I didn't mind. It was all for a good cause. Sincere recorded his last song for the album and everyone wanted to celebrate. They were poppin' bottles, poppin' pills, and dancing all over the place. I took a hit of the blunt and a few shots of D'usse and was lit. I was dancing all over Sincere and he was loving it. I kept seeing the other girls in the studio give me dirty looks. They wanted the attention of the superstar, but he was taken, so they had to settle for the other niggas in the room.

* * *

SINCERE WAS SPEEDING ON THE HIGHWAY IN A NIPSEY BLUE Ferrari. I felt so good and so free.

He turned off the music and looked at me. "Keiks, I need to talk to you," Sincere said, seriously.

I love the nickname *Keiks*, it sounds good coming out of his mouth. I looked at him.

"Okay, bae, what's up?"

"I know it hasn't been a long time, but we've been kickin' it heavy. And I'm feeling the fuck outta you, ma. I want you to be my woman." He stared into my eyes.

This was music to my ears, and this is all that I've ever wanted since meeting him. "I'll be your woman, and anything else you want me to be, baby."

I had a big smile on my face. We both leaned in at the same time for a kiss. Sincere and I were officially a couple, who would've ever thought. Lil' ol' me was in a relationship with a rap star who millions and millions of people love, admire, and want. We were definitely going to be the new hottest couple on the block.

* * *

I JUMPED UP OUT OF MY SLEEP THINKING THAT I HAD PISSED on Sincere's bed, but someone pushed me back down. I couldn't see clearly, but it felt like someone was eating my pussy. My vision adjusted to the dark room, and I was able to make out the figure between my legs. Sincere was hungrily eating me out. My pussy was so damn wet, and I wondered how long he had been doing it.

"I... couldn't help...myself, Keiks. Baby... I need... this pussy...in my mouth," Sincere said as he licked every inch of my pussy.

"Baby... mmhm..." He had me moaning and shaking.

I was going to have an orgasm soon. My whole insides got warm and a sensation that I couldn't explain took over my body.

"I'm cummin' daddy..."

I spread my legs wider for Sincere. His mouth went straight to my hole and sucked out all of my juices. I couldn't stop shaking. Sincere laid next to me and held me until my body calmed down. Next thing I know, I heard my man snoring in my ear. I smiled, kissed him, and took my ass back to sleep.

CHAPTER 14

*S*incere had me staying in New York longer than I had expected. I wasn't even trippin'. I was having the time of my life. He was working on the finishing touches for his album release party and I was busy shopping. He was buying me all kinds of designer shit. I had shit that wasn't even out yet. We were staying in his third home in New York, and this one was just as beautiful as the other two I'd been to. This one was a five bedroom condo, and everything in there was all black. It was giving me grown and sexy vibes.

Sincere had good taste. I was loving everything about him. Yesterday, he surprised me with three Cartier bracelets, a gold, rose gold, and a white gold one. He was spoiling me with gifts, and I was accepting them with open arms. I was finally in a real relationship and couldn't be happier. He kept my pockets laced and kept me eating well. He had all the fame in the world; he was extremely wealthy, and he was eating and beating my pussy up with that bomb ass dick. I was satisfied. I didn't need dick from any other nigga, and I damn sure didn't need their money. My man had it all and then some.

"Aye Keiks, where you at, babe?" Sincere shouted out in the condo.

I was in the bathroom getting ready for Sincere's release party. This is going to be a big night for multiple reasons. He was releasing an album that was going to be his biggest one yet. Also, he was introducing me to the world as his woman. The paparazzi were going to have a field day with us as soon as we stepped into the party.

"I'm in the master bathroom, baby!" I yelled loud enough for him to hear me.

He stood in the bathroom doorway admiring me. "You so fucking bad, ma."

He walked over to me and rubbed his hands all over my body. I was wearing a lime green sheer mini dress with a lime green bra and panty set, and matching Giuseppe Zanotti heels. I put loose curls in my hair and did a natural makeup look on my face.

Sincere gave me a peck on my lips trying not to mess up my makeup. He turned on the shower and removed his clothes. I sat on the black chair that he had in the bathroom and watched him take a shower. The clear shower glass made it easy for me to see the soap suds running down his fit body. I was ready to hop in the shower and make his dick disappear in my mouth.

"Keiks, I want us to go on vacation in Belize, Central America," he said as he washed the soap from his body.

I'd never been to Belize, but I often see photos of IG models out there having a blast. I told myself I was going to go there one day, and now it was my time.

"Hell yeah, I'll go, babe! When are we leaving?"

"We leave in three days, luv. I'll get some luggage delivered here while we're at the club, and I want you to pack our bags tomorrow."

He looked at me through the shower glass and gave me one of his Colgate smiles that I love so much.

"I got you, bae."

I was thrilled that I was going on my first baecation with the man of my dreams. I got up and walked to the bar to pour myself a shot of Bumbu Rum. I looked out into the city lights through the large windows. I was living a dream with my perfect man. Sincere was the type of man I'd been waiting for my whole life. Bitches were going to hate me even more, and niggas were gonna wish they were in Sincere's shoes.

* * *

SINCERE'S SWAG WAS OUT OF THIS WORLD. HE WAS WEARING Dior from head to toe. His black and white attire and the chains that glistened around his neck made him look like a million bucks. My man was fine as fuck, and I was happy to be the woman by his side. We complemented each other, and everyone in the club was going to witness that for themselves.

Sincere and I stepped into the three-story club, hand in hand, and lights were flashing from every spot in the club. My sight started to blur like I was starting to go blind, but thousands were watching so I had to keep it together. No wonder Sincere was wearing his dark Dior sunglasses. I wished he would have warned me because I would've worn my shades as well.

I felt like this is where I belonged. All the attention was on us. Everyone kept coming up to Sincere to either congratulate him, give him daps, hugs, gifts, or interview

him. We weren't even in the club five minutes yet, and there
was so much going on.

We walked to the VIP section, and I sat down while my
man walked around thanking everyone for coming to his
party. I peeped out the scene and noticed that there were
many celebrities in the room. There were actors, basketball
players, football players, baseball players, rappers, singers,
producers, popular social media influencers and so many
more. Sincere was so loved, all these people came out to
support him.

There was a hype man on the stage getting the crowd
ready for the album. I needed a drink badly, so I tried to get
the attention of one of the bottle girls.

"I would like Henny and pineapple juice please," I told
the young bottle girl who was dressed in nothing but a black
thong leotard bodysuit and black platform heels.

I could sense that she had an attitude right off the bat. I
didn't know what the fuck this bitch's problem was. I didn't
know her, but she'd better check that shit real quick.

"Is there a problem?" I asked her.

"Naw, girl, I'll bring the drink in a second." Her snobby
attitude was on level ten.

"Actually, I'm good. I'll get it myself."

I couldn't risk having this bitch drugging me or something, so I took my ass to the bar to do it my damn self. I
was going to tell Sincere about her ass as soon as he came
back to the VIP section.

"Yo! Everybody, listen up. I want to thank y'all from the
bottom of my heart for showing ya boy some love tonight.
And I would like to give a special thanks to my girlfriend,
Keiko Kei. I hope y'all enjoy this album as much as I
enjoyed recording it. Now, DJ, run that shit!" Sincere said
on the stage.

The crowd went crazy. All of a sudden, the spotlight was on me while I stood at the bar waiting for my drink. *What the fuck, how did these muthafuckas find me over here?* There were thousands of people in the club, and they knew exactly where I was. I had to play the role of being a rapper's girlfriend, so I waved and smiled. There it goes again, all of those flashing lights. People were snapping away, and I soaked it all up and enjoyed the moment.

Sincere's album was playing and everyone was loving it. Everybody in the club was dancing. Sincere finally came back to the VIP section to check on me.

"Hey baby, you straight?" he leaned down and asked me.

"I'm good, but I did have one small issue with one of the bottle girls, babe," I told him.

"Which one, and what happened?"

He was starting to sound upset. I looked around for the girl and spotted her in front of one of Sincere's boys, pouting her lips. I pointed her out to Sincere.

"That young one right over there with Jaylanni. I asked her to get me a drink and she gave me major attitude." I pointed at her and I didn't give a fuck who saw.

Sincere didn't even say anything, he left my side and went over to approach the girl. As soon as he walked up to them, I noticed that Jaylanni stepped back, and the girl's eyes lit up when she looked at Sincere. I was not feeling that shit at all, but I sat there watching and waiting to see what was going to happen. Sincere whispered something in her ear, and they both walked away and went into a room that was off to the side of the VIP section.

Oh, fuck no! I know this nigga did not just go into a room with the bitch. I got my ass right up and went in the same direction as they did. I gently turned the knob on the same door they opened not too long ago, and it opened. It was dark and cold in the room and there was a long hallway. I slowly walked down the hall, and I could hear Sincere's voice. They were in another room. I stood to the side, so that they couldn't see me and tried to listen to what Sincere was saying to her.

"Look bitch, we fucked and that was it. That's not my fuckin' baby in yo belly. Now, stay the fuck away from me and my bitch. If I hear or see your ass giving her attitude again, I promise you will regret it. You know what, here! Take this fucking money and get rid of that shit tomorrow, bitch!" Sincere threw the money in her face.

Fuck, I need to get out of here quick before I get caught snooping around. I heard him stop and walk back over to her. I know I probably should've walked my ass right out of that room, but curiosity got the best of me. I wanted to see my man keep checking this bitch. I slowly tiptoed back to the door and peeked in.

Sincere was pulling out his dick. *What the fuck! I know he is not about to fuck this bitch.* I was fucking mad and wanted to march my ass right in that room and fuck him up.

"Suck my dick, bitch!" Sincere shouted at the girl.

She dropped down to her knees and sucked his dick with no hesitation. Sincere grabbed her head with both hands and fucked her mouth like he was fucking a pussy. The bottle girl was choking and gagging on his dick. She tried to push back, but Sincere was not letting up. It made him pump even harder, and her eyes were bulging out of her eye sockets. Then it happened, she threw up all over his dick and clothes.

Sincere looked down and I could see the fire in his eyes. He slapped her so hard she flew across the room.

"I'm so sorry, Sincere. Forgive me, please," she looked terrified.

"Yo stupid ass better be lucky I need to get back to my party."

He pulled out his phone and I assumed that he was texting someone. I took this as an opportunity to get out of there and back to the party. I quickly walked back down the hall out of the door, back to my spot in the VIP Section, and continued sipping on my Henny and pineapple juice. Everyone was still having fun listening to Sincere's songs. No one knew what had just happened on the other side of the door, except for me.

I couldn't believe what I'd just witnessed. My sweet Sincere was acting like a monster in there, but I was sure that he would never treat me like that. Sincere treated me like a Queen. That bitch should have never tried me, or else she wouldn't even be in that situation. And I bet that my man was not the father of that child she was carrying.

I noticed that Jaylanni was carrying a bag, walking to the same room that I had just left. He looked around before entering the room. Jaylanni was Sincere's right-hand man, so he would cover up everything for him.

All eyes were on me, so I sat there dancing in my seat and drinking. Fifteen minutes later, Sincere was walking through the door in a fresh new Dior outfit. I watched him walk out like nothing happened. He sat down next to me and kissed me. I tasted the toothpaste on his tongue. Just like that, my insides were melting. I didn't ask him any questions. I was going to forget what I witnessed in that room and act like nothing happened, just like Sincere did.

I was feeling the drink and I was ready to have a good time with the biggest rapper in the world. The song came on that I heard him record in the studio about me, it blasted through the speakers and the club went crazy.

"Follow me to the stage, baby."

He got up and guided me toward the stage. All eyes were glued on us. The DJ gave him the mic, and he rapped the lyrics to me on stage in front of thousands of people. I was blushing and smiling so hard. I danced my ass off and gave the world a show. People were shouting out and enjoying the performance. I felt powerful as fuck on stage with Sincere. We were meant for each other.

CHAPTER 15

*O*ur things were packed in the Louis Vuitton luggage sets that Sincere purchased for us. We were ready for our baecation. Sincere told me that we would be flying private to Belize. It would be just us and a flight crew that he hired for the trip on the plane. That was alright with me because I hated being on the plane with rude and smelly people.

After Sincere's album release party, the internet was going crazy. Our photos were circulating all over social media, gossip sites, blogs, vlogs, and magazines. This is a different type of stardom that I could get accustomed to. Sincere was used to this, but this is a new kind of fame for me and always how I imagined my life would be.

I know Siana was hearing all about me and seeing my face all over. I bet her bum ass nigga, Zay, wasn't half the man as Sincere. I was living a glamorous life, and she was probably doing the same shit she was doing before, living a boring ass life.

"You ready, baby? The driver is waiting for us." Sincere

walked further into the room interrupting me from my thoughts.

I looked around to make sure I wasn't forgetting anything. "Yeah. I'm ready, bae."

Sincere grabbed our things and out the door we went. We pulled up to a private airport and the driver drove us right in front of the stairs that led up to the airplane doors. I felt like royalty, and we looked the part. The flight crew greeted us like we were Kings and Queens. This is boss shit.

The inside of the airplane looked like a luxury hotel room. There were beds, recliner chairs, TVs, laptops, a full kitchen, and separate rooms for the crew members and us.

"Keiks baby, come here."

Sincere was smoking weed and leaned back in the recliner. He wore red sweats, a wife beater, and red Gucci slides. I swear, everything this man wore looked good on him.

I was sitting in the other recliner seat in front of him. I got up and sat on his lap.

"You are the woman I've been missing in my life, ma. I love you." He stared deeply into my eyes.

I paused. He was finally saying the words I'd been feeling and wanting to say all along. I put my hand on the side of his face and stared deeply into his hazel eyes.

"I love you too, baby." I meant every word.

After he finished smoking, he rubbed my smooth legs. I was wearing a jean skirt, so it was easy access for him. He moved his hands up and massaged my pussy through my thong. I felt my juices seeping through. Sincere slid it to the side and ran his fingers through my slit. One finger went into my pussy, and then a second finger went in. I slowly started to hump his fingers while he finger fucked me. His fingers were wet and he was staring at me with low eyes.

His thumb massaged my clit while his fingers went to work in my pussy.

When I came, his fingers slipped out of me and went right into his mouth. Sincere licked my pussy juice off his fingers and never took his eyes off me. He was turning me on with his freaky ass. It was now my turn to return the favor and make him feel good.

I pulled out his dick and sat right on it, raw. We've always used protection up until this point. He didn't stop me, instead, he pulled me down even more on his thick pole. I bounced, grinded, gyrated, and rode the dick like it was the end of the world. We had sex for hours on that plane and it was the best ride I'd ever had.

* * *

THE CAPTAIN'S VOICE THROUGH THE INTERCOM WOKE US UP. He was letting us know that we were landing in Belize. We got out of bed and went to sit in the recliner seats. It was a smooth landing, and I was happy to see what Belize was all about.

We exited the plane where the humidity was high. Sincere and I were immediately sweating our asses off.

"Shit ma, it's hot as fuck out here. I'm happy I changed into these shorts. This heat got my balls sweating like a muthafucka," Sincere said as we walked toward the customs area.

"Fuck ya balls, bae. My asshole sweating."

We both laughed, and he playfully pulled me closer to him and kissed me. After dealing with customs, we were led back into the airport to take a private jet to Placencia, Belize. It was the island where we would be staying for our trip.

The private plane that Sincere booked was beautiful inside, but it wasn't as luxurious as the private jet that brought us. I was nervous as shit to fly in this much smaller plane. It was going to be a forty-five minute ride, and Sincere promised to hold my hand the whole way there.

When we landed in Placencia at a small airport, I was elated. We made it safely, and I was finally able to breathe a sigh of relief. I looked at Sincere who was calm like he didn't have a care in the world.

A driver was waiting for us when we exited the jet. I was happy to feel the AC blasting. We drove through the beautiful island. Everything was so tropical. Locals were hanging out in boats, riding bikes, and tourists explored the island. People were selling knickknacks, fresh fruits, fresh vegetables, and refreshing drinks on the side of the road.

We pulled up to a long wooden bridge that extended over the water. I looked and noticed that the bridge led to a house across the water. I was happy and afraid at the same time. My ass couldn't swim, so what if this shit fell in the water. I had to calm my nerves and enjoy my time. The driver wheeled our luggage across the bridge and into the house. Sincere and I walked behind him.

When we walked into the house, it was beautiful. All of my fears faded away. The house had two bedrooms, two bathrooms, a living room, a kitchen, and a mini pool and Jacuzzi on the patio that overlooked the ocean. The sliding glass door was the perfect touch. We would be able to slide it open and look out into the ocean while getting a fresh breeze and enjoying the amazing view.

"What'chu think, Keiks?" Sincere looked at me.

"Babe, this is beautiful, I love it! It's the perfect getaway. Thank you, baby."

I was too excited. The kitchen had everything that we

needed. I opened the refrigerator and there were sliced mangos, watermelon, guava, grapes, coconut, and other exotic fruits that I was not familiar with. We had freshly squeezed orange juice, lemonade, different Fanta's, water, coconut water, and Belizean Rum.

"Whatever you want to eat, just let me know. I have a chef coming over in a few hours to cook for us." Sincere gave me a list of the different Belizean cuisines that I could choose from.

I looked at the food and immediately knew what I wanted the chef to make for us. I wanted stew beans, white rice, oxtails, and plantains. My palate couldn't wait for this delicious food. For dessert, we were going to have coconut tarts. I grabbed two glasses for Sincere and myself. I poured the Belizean Rum over ice and we went to sit in the living room.

"I can't imagine experiencing this with anyone else, Sincere. I feel like I've died and gone to heaven," I said in a serious tone.

"You don't ever have to worry, Keiks baby. From now on, all of your experiences will be with me. After you finish your drink, put your bathing suit on."

"Okay baby, I need to shower first. We've been traveling for hours."

I got up and walked into the bedroom to get my body wash before making my way to the bathroom. Sincere walked in the bathroom naked. He joined me in the shower. He washed my whole body, and I washed his. After we were done, we dried off and went back into the bedroom. I slipped into a leopard print, one-piece thong bathing suit with the matching scarf, and Sincere put on his leopard print swim trunks.

We were matching and looking good as fuck. I wanted

to take photos for the Gram. Since our relationship was public now, we didn't care about posting each other. I set up my tripod and mini ring light. Forty pictures later, I was satisfied with our photos. Sincere was a trooper. He posed for all of them.

"It's my turn now. Babe, sit on the edge of the pool right there where the sun is setting. Then look back at me," Sincere pointed to the area where he wanted me to sit.

I did what he said, and he took pictures of me with his phone. "You so fucking bad, ma. How did I get so lucky?" Sincere gassed me up.

"I think I'm the lucky one." I winked at him and continued posing for my man.

"I'm posting this picture on the Gram, and I'm going to caption it, *Queen.*"

He walked over to show me the picture he was going to post of me. My weave was in a bun, my ass was looking good, and Sincere captured my bright smile. I was used to niggas posting me as their WCW all the fucking time, but this is different. Sincere was nothing like those bum niggas. He's who every dude wish they were, a fly boss nigga whom I love so much.

I rushed to get my phone to find my favorite picture of us. In my favorite photo, Sincere was holding me tightly in his arms and we were staring into each other's eyes. I quickly posted it on the Gram and captioned it, *Dreams do come true... #baecation #allmine #belize #instabaddie #handsome #beautiful #powercouple #badbitch*

We put our phones away and continued enjoying each other's company. Sincere and I were playing around in the pool when we heard a knock on the door.

He got out of the pool and dried off quickly before walking to the front door. I looked into the house from the pool to see who was interrupting our alone time. I couldn't hear what they were saying, but I did notice that it was a woman.

I turned back around facing the ocean and enjoyed the light breeze that blew on my face.

Splash!

Sincere jumped in the pool knowing damn well that I didn't want to get my hair wet. I shot him a look and he swam closer to me.

"Chill babe, we on vacation. I'll find someone to redo your hair tomorrow if it's that important."

"I guess you're right, bae. I'll survive, but you know you can't be getting a Black woman's weave wet." I playfully punched his arm.

"I know... I know. My fault, beautiful," he laughed.

"By the way, who was that at the door?"

"Oh, that's the chef. I told her what you want her to cook for dinner, so she's about to cook it for us."

"Yay! I can't wait!" I clapped my hands together excitedly.

We spent the whole time joking around in the pool while the chef cooked. I smelled the aroma of the Belizean food and my mouth watered and my stomach growled.

The chef walked over to the pool to let us know dinner was ready. I turned to face her, getting a closer look. She is beautiful. She looks like she is Indian and Black. One thing that I noticed when we landed in Belize is that the Belizean people came in many different shades and sizes, and some of them had exotic features. The chef was no different, her brown sugar skin tone and long jet black flowy hair made her stand out.

She walked back to the kitchen and started washing the dishes. Sincere got out of the pool first, then helped me get out too. I trailed behind him into the bedroom. We were both looking like shriveled up prunes from being in the water for so long.

Sincere turned on the shower and told me to get in with him, I obliged. Seeing my man standing there naked made me ready to feel him deep inside my pussy. I got closer to him and began sucking on his neck. Not long after, his hard dick poked my stomach.

"Come on Keiks, let's go eat before the food gets cold. There will be enough time for that later," he assured.

"Okay," I pouted. I wanted the dick right fucking now.

We dried off our damp skin and changed into matching silk robes. There was no need for clothes because they will be coming off later anyway.

I no longer heard any movement in the kitchen and momentarily thought the chef had departed. We walked into the kitchen and there stood the chef, naked as the day she was born.

"What the fuck is this!" I shouted out.

She didn't even budge. I looked at Sincere; he was staring her down with lust in his eyes. I couldn't believe this shit.

"Baby, it's okay. I hired Chef Tessa to cook for us, and to do some other thangs for us too," he said with a broad smile.

I was furious. *Why the fuck does he think I would want another bitch here with us.* I was all that he needed. Instead of poppin' off like I wanted to, I was going to save that shit for later. I didn't want to ruin our baecation, but I was pissed.

I glanced at Chef Tessa, and she gave me a smirk. I wanted to knock that shit right off of her face. I went from starving to having no appetite, but I needed to put something on my stomach.

I didn't even want to eat the food that this bitch made. Sincere was gobbling down his food and staring at Chef Tessa's naked body on the patio. When he wasn't looking, I was rolling my eyes at him so damn hard that if I didn't stop, my eyes would've probably ended up getting stuck.

We finished our food, and Sincere anxiously went into the bathroom to wash his hands and brush his teeth. I hesitantly did the same in the second bathroom. I really didn't want to be next to him right now.

When I finally exited the bathroom and went into the living room, I was ready to kill both Chef Tessa and Sincere. He was sitting on the couch, legs wide open, while Chef Tessa slurped and sucked his dick.

Sincere noticed me standing there and signaled me over. I slowly walked over to them and dropped to my knees. I was not about to have this bitch outdo me in sucking my man's dick.

I tried to push her out of the way, but she was a little stronger than I thought. She sucked Sincere's dick even harder. I looked up at him and wished I could slap the fucking smile off of his face.

Since this hoe wasn't stopping, I lowered my head and put Sincere's balls into my mouth. He was grunting like I'd never heard him do before. I was angry, but I was not about to let no hoe ass bitch see me sweat.

I got up and removed my robe. I could see Chef Tessa look up and stare at my body. *Yeah, bitch!* I got on the couch and stood over Sincere. I sat my pussy right on his mouth, and his tongue went to work, licking all over my pussy.

I looked behind to see what Chef Tessa was doing because I didn't hear her slurping on Sincere's dick anymore. She was covering his dick with a condom. *Ugh,* I was furious. She plopped her ass right on Sincere's lap and his dick disappeared into her pussy.

"Mmmm..."

Chef Tessa was moaning and riding my man like there was no tomorrow. This made me ride his face aggressively. His hands cupped my ass tightly and he helped guide my pussy all over his face.

"Oooo, daddy... Yes..."

He was eating me out so good that for a minute I forgot that it wasn't just us in the room. The faster Chef Tessa rode Sincere's dick, the faster his tongue flicked in and out of my pussy. This shit was feeling amazing, but I still couldn't shake the feeling that another bitch was getting my man's dick right there in front of me. That was my dick, and it was about time that I claimed my shit.

"Move!" I pushed her off of Sincere as soon as I noticed that she was about to have an orgasm.

"Keiks, yo what the fuck!" Sincere looked at me like I was crazy, and I looked at him the same.

I removed the condom with the tip of my fingers and made up my face in disgust as I tossed it to the side.

I hopped on the dick and showed little Ms. Chef how it's done. I had my back turned to Sincere, so that he could see my ass bouncing up and down on his dick. He was gripping the fuck out of my waist.

Chef Tessa must have gotten tired of not getting any action, so once again she dropped down to her knees in front of us. At this point, I wasn't even mad any more. Sincere's dick was feeling so good in my pussy, I didn't even care what was going on around us until her hair brushed against my pussy. I looked down and she was licking on Sincere's balls that were covered in my juices. I didn't stop riding him. Before I knew it, she was sucking on my clit.

Having Sincere's dick filling up my pussy and getting my pearl tongue sucked on drove me insane. I came so damn hard, and my man was right behind me causing our cum to flow out and right into Chef Tessa's mouth.

Sincere and I were slumped and too exhausted to move. I kept my eyes on Chef Tessa though, because I didn't know what she was about to do next. She got up, put on her clothes, and stood in front of us.

"It was a pleasure serving you two."

She winked at us before walking out of the front door. I looked at Sincere and just that fast, he was leaning back on the couch snoring. I got up to shut the sliding patio door. Then I found a spot next to Sincere on the couch and drifted off to sleep.

CHAPTER 16

*I*t'd been two weeks and Sincere and I were living it up in Belize. After our little situation with Chef Tessa, I was happy that Sincere didn't pull any other bullshit stunts during our trip. We went snorkeling, partied with the locals, ate well, and fucked all over that damn island. I was going to miss being in Belize. We had so much fun together, and this trip solidified that Sincere is the man for me.

We posted our pictures on social media, and the internet was going crazy. People were showing us mad love, but of course, we had our haters as well. I was getting called a gold digger, a groupie, a hoe, etc. I didn't give a fuck, I was living the life millions of people wanted to live. After a while, I got tired of clapping back and stopped reading the comments. I posted even sexier photos, and the likes were going up like crazy. My followers had even increased since being with Sincere. I have over ten million followers now. Being with Sincere came with so much fame and perks. I was loving my life and loving my man even more.

We enjoyed every second, minute, hour, day, and week with each other. Now, it was time for us to take our asses back to the United States. I packed up our bags while Sincere made sure our flights were arranged and situated.

We were going to take another private jet to the airport in Belize City, and then take a private plane back to Los Angeles. I wasn't looking forward to stepping foot on that private jet, but I needed to get over it fast. I took two shots of Hennessy Pure White and walked closely behind Sincere as we walked across the bridge to the truck where the driver waited for us on the other end.

I took in the beauty of Placencia one more time as we drove to the airport. Our baecation was definitely a success. It started off a little rocky, but it turned out to be perfect. I didn't care what anyone said, being with a popular, rich, nigga was the best thing in my life. I was getting all of the fame that I've ever wanted. I had my own money that I didn't even have to touch because my man handled everything financially. The glamorous life was meant to be mine.

* * *

WE LANDED IN LOS ANGELES, AND I WAS FEELING GOOD AND well-rested. We were tired from all the partying in Belize and slept the whole way back. Thank God for the private plane. We slept comfortably without any interruptions.

"Babe, thanks so much for an amazing trip," I beamed, happiness written all over my face.

"No problem. You know I got you, ma," Sincere gently kissed my lips.

Sincere's driver was waiting for us when we landed. We

avoided the paparazzi, and I was happy about that because I looked crazy. I didn't need any bad pictures of me floating around. Trolls would have a field day clowning my ass.

"Keiks, I want you to stay with me tonight."

"Alright, baby. I will." *Shit, I had no plans of going back to my place tonight anyway, so that is cool with me.*

We pulled up to the same house where I first met Sincere at his surprise birthday party. I smiled at the memories. I scooted closer to him and laid my head on his shoulder. Life is perfect.

* * *

"AYO MA!" SINCERE RUSHED INTO THE MOVIE THEATER room that was in his house.

This man had a whole movie theater, an arcade, a studio, indoor gym with a large basketball court, a club, and bowling alley all built inside of his mansion. There are twelve bedrooms and twelve bathrooms. I don't know how I didn't see all of this when I was here for his birthday party. This is a glasshouse, but these rooms were built underground, hidden from the outside. Everything about his home screamed luxury. I was once gushing over the Galores house, and now here I am in a home that was even better than the Galores.

"Yes, babe?" I paused the movie and looked at him.

"Prolific Vibez Magazine wants us to be on the cover of their magazine this month," he said.

My eyes opened big. This is major. Prolific Vibes Magazine is one of the biggest magazines in the world. All of the biggest celebrities were featured in their magazine, and now I'm going to be on the cover with Sincere. *Who would've ever thought?* I got up and jumped for joy. Sincere laughed at my craziness.

"Are you serious, babe?"

He was as serious as a heart attack, but I still made sure that this was really happening.

"Yeah, Keiks. They want us to shoot next week."

Words couldn't describe how excited I was. I wanted to call someone to tell them the good news, then I remembered I really didn't have any friends anymore. Siana, Joe, and Keith were no longer in my life. I got sad for a moment thinking about them, but it didn't last long because I had everything that I needed right here next to me. I leaned over, parted my lips, and passionately kissed Sincere.

He returned the kiss and pulled me closer to his body. He tugged at my boy shorts until they fell down to my ankles. I removed my sports bra and proceeded to remove his basketball shorts. His dick was nice and hard, just the way I like it. I massaged his dick in my hands while kissing his chest. His dick was throbbing in my hands. It was time to feel his dick throbbing inside my pussy.

I dropped down to my knees and spit on his dick to get it nice and wet. Sincere got down on his knees and laid me on the thick carpet in the theater room. I spread my legs and anticipated the sensation that was coming.

As always, Sincere did not disappoint. He beat the fuck out of my pussy. I was squirting all over his dick, leaving a puddle on the carpet. *Damn, this man fucks me so good. I don't ever want to let this dick go.* I am addicted to Sincere just as much as I am addicted to money and social media. This man is a keeper.

* * *

IT IS THE DAY OF THE PHOTOSHOOT FOR PROLIFIC VIBEZ Magazine, and I was dancing around while I packed a small bag of essential things that I might need. Most of my things were now at Sincere's mansion. I went to my condo twice to grab some of my things, and I hadn't been home since. He wanted me to spend most of my time at his place, so that's what I did.

Sincere was at a meeting with his crew. He told me to be ready in two hours, so I wanted to be ready when he arrived.

Buzz! Buzz!

My cell phone vibrated on the nightstand next to the bed. I rushed over to see who was calling. I smiled when I saw *Bae* flash across the screen, it was Sincere calling.

"Hey Bab—" I paused and pressed my ear closer to the phone.

"Fuck Sincere, you fuck me so good, daddy… ooo…" I heard an unfamiliar voice say on the other end.

"Take… this… fucking… dick!" Sincere said.

"Hello! Sincere! Sincere! What the fuck!" I yelled into the phone as tears formed in my eyes. *I know this nigga is not fucking a bitch while he is supposed to be at a meeting!*

I heard someone fumbling with the phone, then heard it click.

I stood in Sincere's room fuming. My "perfect" man was fucking another bitch while I was at his mansion, waiting for us to go to a couples shoot for a magazine. I was so fucking livid, I couldn't even focus anymore.

This nigga got me fucked up, do he not know who the fuck I am. I'm the baddest bitch, and he got the nerve to cheat on me. I was going to let his ass have it as soon as he walked through these doors.

I grabbed my packed bag and made my way to the

front of the house. I was going to wait for his trifling ass at the front door.

Two hours later, Sincere came strolling into the house, smiling. "Hey ma, you ready?"

I looked at him with fire in my eyes. "Nigga, where the fuck were you!"

I got in his face and pointed my finger in it.

"Keiks, stop pointing in my face," he said in a serious tone.

"Or else what?" I shot back.

"Keep pointing yo fucking finger in my face and yo ass gon' find out," he challenged.

I shoved my finger into his forehead. "I heard yo stupid ass fuckin' some bitch, Sincere. How could you!"

"So what. You my main bitch. And I fuck different hoes from time to time."

He shrugged his shoulders and walked down the hall.

I followed right behind. "So, if I fuck other niggas, would that be cool with you?"

Bam!

Sincere pushed me hard into the wall, and I hit my arm. I knew there was going to be a bruise.

"If you ever let another man touch you, I will beat yo ass, Keiko. Don't fucking play with me!" he shouted as he walked into the bathroom.

I leaned on the wall, holding my arm while trying to process what the fuck just went wrong. Fifteen minutes later, Sincere walked out of the bathroom with a towel wrapped around his waist. I stared at him wondering what happened to my sweet Sincere.

I walked back to the front door and sat on the couch. I didn't even feel like going to this shoot anymore. Sincere walked into the living room looking and smelling good. At this moment, I hate that I love him so much.

"Come on. Let's go. I don't want to be late."

He grabbed my bag and walked out of the front door. Sincere acted like he didn't push me into the wall not too long ago. Instead of going off on him, I quickly sat in the passenger seat of his black-on-black Beamer. I was still shocked about what had transpired, so I sat in silence.

We pulled into a parking lot, and I looked around to see where we were. There was nothing around the large warehouse building.

"Before we walk in there, you need to get your shit together. Walk in there and act like you're fucking happy," he demanded.

I didn't say a word. I opened the door to get out, and Sincere pulled me back inside the car. "Did you hear what I just said Keiko?"

I nodded my head and snatched my arm out of his tight grip. I slammed the door behind me. Sincere got out of the car, and I could tell he was pissed. He walked over to the area where I was standing and leaned in real close to my face like he was going to kiss me.

"Bitch, don't let me beat your fucking ass in this parking lot. Now, act right," he said through clenched teeth.

I was a little fearful because the look on his face told me that I'd better not play with him.

We walked into the building, hand in hand. The inside looks nothing like the outside. Different themes are set up around the building. There are themes for a Barbie shoot, '70s club, luxury bedroom, beach, pink room, royal blue room, black room, green room, and red room. They have various scenes for everything you could think of. I wonder which room we are going to taking our photos.

I heard a familiar voice behind me, and when I turned around, I almost shit my pants.

"Welcome! The hottest couple around. You two look amazing!" Mrs. Galore stood in front of us with a big smile on her face.

Sincere smiled at her and even though I was in no mood to smile, I still gave her a fake smile.

What the fuck is she doing here? I wondered if Sincere knew about my association with the Galores.

"Keiko, it's great to see you again," Mrs. Galore gave me a hug.

My heart was beating fast because I didn't know what was going on.

"You two know each other?" Sincere questioned. He looked back and forth between me and Mrs. Galore.

"Yes. Keiko modeled for my new collection."

"I feel it. You do it all, Mrs. Galore. You have a clothing company and you have a partnership with Prolific Vibez Magazine," Sincere said to Mrs. Galore.

"Yes, I do. Okay, I won't hold you two up. I just wanted to say hello before I head out. And congrats on making the cover of our magazine. When they told me who would be on this month's cover, I was ecstatic. Well, I must go now," Mrs. Galore cheerfully said.

She gave us a quick hug, and when she walked away, she brushed my ass with her hand when Sincere turned to look at the man who was walking toward us.

This bold bitch was crazy. If she only knew, the way that Sincere was acting today he would probably beat her ass and mine too if he would've caught her touching me.

"Hello Sincere and Keiko, please follow me," the White man said and hurriedly walked ahead of us.

We followed him into the makeup room. There was a

full glam squad in here. He sat me in the chair and did the same to Sincere. We had different individuals tending to us to help prepare us for our shoot.

Sincere and I should have won an acting award the way we were acting and carrying on like we were the happiest couple in the room. The team fell in love with us. It was crazy how everyone was acting like we were so perfect, and shit, I felt the same before today. It's true when they say looks are deceiving. Sincere was hugging and kissing on me. I smiled and giggled, but I really wanted to push his ass off of me.

After my hair and makeup were done, a stylist entered the room with a rack filled with designer clothes. They wanted me to wear a beautiful, gold, long, backless gown, and Sincere was going to wear a black suit, white dress shirt, and gold tie. My hair was pinned up with a few loose curls that flowed down the side of my face, and Sincere had a fresh line up. We changed into our outfits and everyone's eyes lit up when we walked out of the room.

"Wow! You two look amazing!" a man holding a camera shouted. I assumed that he was the photographer.

I couldn't lie, we looked damn good together. I couldn't keep my eyes off him, and I know he was feeling the same because he hadn't stopped staring at me since we left the room.

The photographer and glam crew escorted us down the hall into a room that was set up like a luxurious living room. Everything was white in the room, except for the gold and black decorations that were placed throughout the set. It matched our attire well.

For the next two hours, we posed and posed, while others looked on admiring the *perfect couple*.

At the last minute, they decided that we were going to

be included inside of the magazine as well, so they wanted a few sexy photos for that too. We walked into a room that looked like a bedroom. I was ready to get the shoot over with.

I wore red lace lingerie and Sincere would be naked. My body would cover his dick, so that he wouldn't be too exposed in the magazine. The way the photographer positioned us was perfect. It was a sexy shoot, but we made it look tasteful. The whole time the camera was snapping away, I couldn't stop hearing the woman's voice when Sincere's phone accidentally called me earlier. I kept replaying it over and over again in my head. I was starting to get angry again, but I had to keep it together until our photo shoot was over.

"Alright guys, that's a wrap. These pictures came out great. This might be one of the best magazine covers I've ever shot," the photographer said, excitedly.

Sincere and I thanked everyone before we called it a day and left the premises. I was exhausted and wanted to just crawl in bed and go to sleep. We got inside the car, and I leaned my head back and closed my eyes until Sincere roughly grabbed my face.

"What the fuck was up with that old bitch touching your ass?"

Fuck, how did he see that shit? I thought he was looking the other way.

"What? A cat got your fucking tongue?"

I was speechless, and I was not in the fucking mood to explain that shit. I signed that contract with the Galores and there was no telling what would occur if I ever got caught saying what happened. To be honest, at this point, I was more afraid of what Sincere will do if he finds out.

"Babe, I think it was an accident. That old woman is harmless."

"You betta not be lying to me, Keiko."

"I promise, I'm not lying."

For the rest of the ride back to Sincere's house, I didn't say another word and neither did he. My mind was all over the place. Just that fast, things had shifted, and I was starting to doubt my relationship with Sincere. Hopefully, this crazy side of him will change soon. I just couldn't give up this glamorous life easily.

CHAPTER 17

*O*ver the next few weeks, I was on an emotional rollercoaster. My relationship turned toxic as fuck. One minute we loved each other deeply and the next minute we hated each other. The arguments always ended with Sincere putting his hands on me. I had turned into his very own personal punching bag.

I was feeling lost and confused. I was slowly losing myself, but I couldn't leave Sincere. Every time he whooped my ass, he would bring me back flowers, expensive jewelry, designer clothes, shoes, bags, or cars. He would give me stacks of money, fuck my brains out, and then, I would forgive him. He promised me that he wouldn't put his hands on me anymore. He broke that promise every time.

Sincere made me move in with him, claiming he couldn't sleep without me every night. So, I packed up my things, rented out my condo, and moved in with my man.

I was excited that I would be living in his big ass mansion, but that excitement quickly faded. After his album went platinum, bitches were constantly throwing the pussy at him, and he was catching it every single time. His cheating was worse than ever, and if I said anything about it, all hell would break loose.

One thing we didn't stop doing was posting pictures of each other on our social media pages. We portrayed being perfect on the internet, and to everyone, we were the happiest couple in the world. Behind closed doors, no one knew what was really going on. People were tagging us as relationship goals, perfect couple, soulmates, lovers, best friends, and a bunch of other shit. Women were envious of me and wished they were in my shoes just from looking at our photos and videos on the internet. No one would be able to see the pain in my eyes by looking at our social media pages. We were fucking frontin' for the Gram.

We were getting booked for magazines, events, and interviews. Sincere and I always walked into a building hand in hand, smiling from ear to ear, and giving each other googly eyes whenever other people were around. These people had no idea we had just argued or fought right before stepping foot in those doors. We were faking it big time; I couldn't let people know that my life wasn't perfect, and Sincere didn't want to mess up his reputation. So, we learned how to turn the switch on and off.

I was really starting to miss Siana tremendously, but I was still blocked and refused to beg for a friendship that she no longer wanted.

I missed the protection from Joe and Keith and living a carefree life. Nowadays, I could barely move without Sincere being all up in my ass. I needed someone to talk to just to take my mind off of things, and I realized I hadn't talked to StacksMami in a long time. Sincere was in the arcade entertaining his friends, so I grabbed my cell phone and called StacksMami. She answered on the second ring.

"Hello?"

Right off the bat, I could tell that StacksMami didn't sound like her usual cheerful self.

"What's up with you, girl? Are you okay?" I asked nervously.

There was a long pause before StacksMami gave me the shock of my life. "Keiko, I tested positive for HIV, and I'm not doing too well."

My jaw dropped. I didn't know what to say, so I just cried into the phone.

"Keiko, please don't cry for me. I'm gonna pull through. I see you loving and living your life with Sincere. Keep living that shit for me. I'm so happy that you are happy," she said sincerely.

I wanted to yell into the phone and tell her that I'm not fucking happy and that Sincere was cheating on me and beating my ass every chance that he got, but I couldn't find the words.

"Stacks, how did this happen?"

"Remember the night when we went to the swingers club and I competed in that competition? Anyway, some of the guys weren't wearing condoms, and one of them had HIV. I don't even know how many people are infected now, but I did contact Angel. She kept apologizing, and she closed down the club for good. She's been helping me through this," she said in a defeated tone.

"Stacks, I'm so sorry this is happening to you. I'm sorry I didn't stop you that night? I'm sorry I didn't check on you sooner," I cried out into the phone.

I could hear StacksMami sniffling on the other end. "Keiko, it's not your fault. I will be okay. Please live your life to the muthafuckin' fullest... and Keiko, please be safe always. I gotta go take my meds now. And Keiko?"

"Yes, Stacks?"

"I know we weren't the closest, but I just want to say that I love you. Take care," she said with sadness.

"I love you too, girl. Now please, take care of yourself."

I needed to get off the phone quickly because I was starting to feel dizzy. Then all of a sudden, I fell on the floor and everything went dark.

* * *

I WOKE UP IN A BRIGHT WHITE ROOM. I COULD HEAR PEOPLE whispering around me. When my eyes finally adjusted to the light, I was able to see that I was in a hospital.

"Nurse, she's up," Sincere said in a concerned tone.

I tried to remember what happened and it dawned on me that I passed out right after talking to StacksMami. Sadness came over me when I thought about the words she said to me. My heart was aching for her and I couldn't understand why she had to go through that. She was so young and full of life. Just a young woman trying to have fun. The salty tears rolled out of my eyes, down the sides of my face, and onto the pillow.

Sincere leaned over and kissed me on my cheek. He was the last person I wanted to see right now. All of the nurses were in the room catering to the "superstar" Sincere, even though I was one laid up in the bed wondering what the fuck was going on. Sincere sensed my frustration and called the doctor into the room. He must have paid them a pretty penny because the doctor rushed into the room, almost knocking down the nurses.

"Good, you're up. Hello Ms. Konners, I'm Dr. Morton. Your boyfriend brought you in after finding you passed out in your bedroom. After running some tests, we found out that you are expecting. Congratulations," he said with a smile.

Fuck my life! I looked at Sincere and he gave me a smile. He stroked my hair and held my hand gently.

"Keiks, we're having a baby!" he said, excitedly.

This muthafucka is crazy. He was just hitting me last night, and now, he was acting like he was the happiest man in the world. I thought back to our time in Belize and remembered him cumming inside of me. If only I knew what I know now, that would have never happened.

I closed my eyes and acted like I was going back to sleep. I couldn't handle this shit right now. I held my eyes shut until I heard the doctor tell Sincere and the nurses to let me get my rest.

* * *

I WAS BACK AT HOME RELAXING IN BED LOOKING AT ALL OF the photos Sincere and I have taken. We looked so happy and in love in each photo. I fought back tears trying to figure out why things changed between us. Here I was, an Insta-Baddie that many looked up to. Now, I'm hiding from the world because my man who people all around the world love so much is treating me like shit. I knew Sincere was capable of going back to the man that I first met. I just couldn't leave and let another bitch come in and take my place. I was pregnant with a rich nigga's baby, and this is every groupie's dream.

CHAPTER 18

"*B*itch, you are a muthafuckin' liar! Explain this shit!" Sincere screamed as he threw his cell phone at my face.

I was confused. I thought he was slowly changing. Ever since finding out that we are expecting, he was doing the sweetest things for me. It had been a few days, and he hadn't cursed me out or hit me.

I picked up the phone, and I sat on the couch frozen as I stared at the screen. *How the fuck? Who the fuck? What the fuck? Why the fuck?* My mind was going crazy.

On the screen, there was a video of Mrs. Galore eating the fuck out of my asshole while Mr. Galore stood back beating his meat. This was the same day I had my photo-shoot for their clothing line. Someone had a hidden camera and was secretly recording what took place in the room. I was devastated. I wanted to know who the fuck had the audacity to record us, and more importantly, why the fuck did they send Sincere this video.

I looked up at Sincere and thought I was staring into

the eyes of the devil. He charged toward me. I jumped off the couch trying to get away from him, but I was too slow. Sincere grabbed my ankles and dragged me toward him.

"Sincere! Let me go right fuckin' now! I'm fucking pregnant!" I shouted out at the top of my lungs.

I know this nigga is not about to hurt me while I'm carrying his unborn child.

"Since you love getting yo asshole played with, I'ma give you what yo hoe ass love!"

He pulled down my sweatpants and panties, and forcefully positioned me on all fours.

"Sincere! Please don't do this!" I cried and begged.

Sincere grabbed a bottle of Vaseline from the side of the couch that I hadn't seen before and scooped up a handful and rubbed it all over his dick.

Tears flowed out of my eyes as Sincere rammed his dick so far up my ass. I tried to get myself out of his tight grip, but Sincere's strength overpowered mine. After a while, I stopped fighting, but the tears didn't stop.

It felt like my asshole was slowly ripping apart. The more I cried, the harder Sincere pumped in and out of my ass. He was grunting and loving the feeling of my tight asshole.

"Sincere! Please stop! I feel... like I'm about... to shit on myself!" I yelled at him, but he kept pumping faster and harder.

I could tell Sincere was about to bust a nut as he shoved his dick deeper into my dark cave. He pulled out, and I felt the liquid flowing out of my asshole. I looked down at the light brown mixture forming a puddle onto the wood floor. Sincere's cum mixed with my shit was disgusting and it smelled horrible. After the scent hit my nostrils, I threw up everywhere.

"Nasty bitch! Look what you did, clean all this shit up!" Sincere snapped.

He got up, walked away, and disappeared into the long hallway. I laid there on the floor in vomit, shit, and cum. My whole body felt too sore to get up, so I held my stomach and cried until I had no more tears left.

* * *

AFTER THAT SHIT THAT SINCERE PULLED YESTERDAY, I should've packed up my things and left, but I didn't. He left the house and came back home this morning with the biggest flower bouquet I'd ever seen in my life. He even bought me diamond earrings, a diamond necklace, and a diamond bracelet. He apologized over and over for what he did as he held and kissed my stomach.

"Babe, you gotta stop hurting me. I love you," I said sheepishly.

"I'm sorry, Keiks. I know. I just love you so much, and I can't stand someone else having you. I don't wanna lose you, baby."

He wrapped me up in his arms and hugged me. I felt so good in his warm embrace. He slowly guided his hands down to my pussy. Even though I was still sore, I let him remove my pajamas. It had been a while since we actually made love. I was yearning to feel loved again. Sincere picked me up and carried me to our bed. He spread my legs open and slowly placed his mouth between my pussy lips. My back arched a little bit and his tongue continuously licked my clit. I missed feeling him between my legs eating my sweet pussy.

"I love this pussy so much, girl," Sincere said with his head between my thighs.

Sincere showed my clit so much attention. He had my body trembling uncontrollably. I was enjoying the tongue lashing my man was giving me.

"Baby... I'm cummin' for... you..." I moaned and grinded my pussy all over his face.

While I tried to get my breathing together, I felt Sincere slide his big dick inside of my pussy. Damn, it felt so good. I missed him. I missed the feeling he was giving me. He made love to me like never before.

"I love you, Keiks," Sincere said as his dick went deeper into my sweet honey pot.

His dick got harder as my pussy tightly gripped around it. Sincere and I exploded at the same damn time. Our love making session was everything that I needed. This is the Sincere that I love and adore. He held me in his arms, and we fell asleep together.

* * *

I WOKE TO MY CELL PHONE VIBRATING NONSTOP. I LOOKED around and saw that Sincere was still knocked out. I checked the time and it was 10:30pm. Damn, Sincere and I had been sleeping all day. I grabbed my phone and walked into our master bathroom. I needed to pee badly, so while I released my bladder, I looked to see who kept calling me. There were eighty missed calls from a number that I did not recognize. It must've been important because whoever it was, did not let up. The phone started vibrating in my hand again, and it was the same number. Usually, I didn't answer unknown numbers, but this time, I felt like I needed to.

"Hello?" I answered.

"Keiko, oh Keiko thank God you answered!" the person on the other end sounded relieved.

I thought the voice sounded familiar, but I wasn't quite sure who it was. "I'm sorry, who is this?" I asked.

"This is Angel."

My heart started beating rapidly. Why was Angel calling me all damn day? My mind went straight to StacksMami.

"Angel... where is Stacks?" I questioned.

"I'm so sorry, Keiko, she's gone..." Angel broke down crying.

My heart dropped, this couldn't be happening this quickly.

"Ang..." my voice cracked and I couldn't get the words to come out of my mouth.

"She committed suicide today. I left the house to get her some food, and when I came back, she was in the tub. Keiko, she drowned herself in the fucking tub. If I would've known, I would not have left her side," Angel said sadly.

I cried out loud and Angel was on the other end doing the same. I was sprawled out on the bathroom floor feeling and looking a hot mess. Angel and I ended our call. I was left alone thinking about life.

"Baby, what's wrong? Get up," Sincere said, his brows bunched in confusion.

I looked at him with red and swollen eyes. "Bae, I just found out that my friend committed suicide this morning."

Sincere immediately joined me on the bathroom floor and just held me while I cried into his arms. We sat there for thirty minutes, neither one of us saying a word. He comforted me and let me get it all out.

CHAPTER 19

$\mathcal{I}$ was a ball of emotions for the next week. Social media was flooded with messages honoring StacksMami. I posted a picture of us that we took in her car right before we had entered the swingers club. Under the picture I wrote, *Fly High My Angel*. I felt like I was going crazy, feeling like I could have stopped all of this. The only good thing that I was happy about was that Sincere was acting much better. It seemed like his cheating had slowed down too.

Even though I was hurting from StacksMami's death, I finally felt like things at home were back to normal. Sincere and I were loving each other the same way we loved one another in the beginning. He was busy preparing for the Hip Hop Awards that is coming up. He is going to perform at the awards and host the awards after party. In the past, I would be excited as fuck to get all dressed up for the awards because that meant the ballers would be out and I would be getting my pussy beat the fuck up by some rich niggas. Now, my life was totally different. Even though I had my baller nigga and more money than I could ever think of, my soul still felt empty. I was grieving and taking Stacks death hard, but I had to get it together for my unborn child.

I have a little pudge now, and I am still surprised that there is a little life growing inside me. I didn't even get a chance to tell Stacks that I'm going to be a mother. I know she would want me to be happy, so I am going to honor her and do just that. Her funeral is coming up, but I cannot attend. I didn't want my last memories of her to be at her funeral. I ordered a large flower arrangement that is going to be delivered to the funeral home, and I anonymously sent $40,000 to her family. On my own time, I would visit her grave, but I just can't do it now.

* * *

SINCERE HIRED A WHOLE GLAM CREW TO COME TO OUR home and help me get ready for the Hip Hop Awards. I am wearing a blue, mini, Tom Ford dress that is hugging my curves and Christian Louboutin's heels the same color as my dress. My body is draped in diamonds, they are all "sorry" gifts that Sincere had bought me. For my hair, I wore a short blonde bob. The glam crew hooked me up from head to toe. I'm feeling like my old self and ready to be the muthafuckin' show stopper. I cannot wait for Sincere to see me looking like the bad bitch that I am.

I was dressed and waiting for Sincere to come back to the house to get me. I heard the front door open, and my man stood in the doorway looking good enough to eat. His suit and shoes matched my dress perfectly. I ran into his arms and hugged him tightly. He pulled back away from me and made me do a spin so that he could get a good look at me.

"Damn, my baby is looking beautiful," he said, seductively.

"Thank you, bae. So are you."

I blushed and pulled him in for a kiss. I was admiring his sexy ass from head to toe.

Instead of getting a driver to take us to the awards, Sincere thought it would be best to drive us himself in his blue Porsche. I didn't complain. I just chilled in the passenger seat as Roddy Ricch's voice blasted through the car speakers.

* * *

SINCERE AND I WALKED THE RED-CARPET HOLDING HANDS. We smiled and posed as we stopped for pictures. There were flashes from the cameras going off from every angle. There were celebrities all over the place. It felt good to feel important. Everyone tried to stop us for a quick interview or to take a picture. I had all the fame that I ever wanted, and then some.

We found our seats on the front row right next to a few other popular rappers, and their wives or girlfriends. We greeted each other, but I stayed to myself after that. I could tell that the women felt a way about me from the way they glared at me. Either they had a problem with me, or they wanted my man. Either way, I was not about to let these bitches get under my skin.

"Keiks, you good? I gotta go backstage to get ready for my performance. If you want, you can come back there with me," Sincere said.

"I'll stay here, babe. I want to be front and center for your performance." I smiled at him.

He leaned down to kiss me, and I swear I heard one of

them hating bitches sucked their teeth. That just made me smile at Sincere even harder. Sincere's performance was first and everybody was out of their seats dancing, even me. He performed his hit songs, and people were rapping to the lyrics. Some were waving their hands in the air, swaying their hips and groupies were gyrating their ass all down the aisle trying to get Sincere or other rappers to notice them. I kept cutting my eyes at a big booty bitch who made her way from the back all the way to the front row. She was doing the most. I almost tripped her when she sashayed her stupid ass right in front of me. I looked around for some type of security to take this bitch to the back.

Security finally arrived and escorted her to the back where she belonged. Now, I was able to focus on my man. He was staring at me from the stage, and I started feeling all warm inside. *Fuck, I love this man.* I forgot all about the bad shit we'd been through. In my heart I knew that Sincere loved me unconditionally; he just had a weird way of showing it sometimes.

After his performance, Sincere came back to sit next to me. We sat there and enjoyed the rest of the show. They were now going to announce the winner for the best album of the year.

"And the winner is… Sincere!" the host announced, and the crowd erupted.

Sincere was smiling hard. He gave me a kiss and whispered for me to walk on the stage with him.

I could feel the eyes that were piercing through my back. I kept my composure, smiled brightly, and strutted my pretty ass right up to the stage with my man.

"Wow! Thank y'all. Man, God is good. I would like to thank God, my crew, my fans, my woman Keiko, and my unborn baby."

Sincere held up his award with one hand, and with the other hand, he held my belly. The crowd went ballistic. I looked out into the crowd with a smile on my face. Women were whispering to their friends, men were staring at me with desire, some looked genuinely happy for us, and others looked with jealousy in their eyes.

We exited the stage and were led to the backstage area. There were people everywhere. A photographer approached us and congratulated both Sincere and myself before he started snapping away.

Once we were alone, I looked over at Sincere. "Baby, I'm so proud of you. I know how hard you worked on this album, and all of the sleepless nights were all worth it."

I wrapped my arms around his neck and gave him a big hug.

Sincere smiled at me. "Thank you, beautiful, you don't know how much that means to me."

He grabbed my hand and we walked down a hall where all the celebrity dressing rooms were located. We stopped in front of the door labeled *SINCERE* in bold black letters. We went inside of the room and Sincere went straight to the glass table. I couldn't really see what he was doing from where I stood, so I slowly walked behind him.

This nigga was getting ready to snort a line of coke. *This is why his ass been trippin' as much as he's been.* I was furious. *How long has he been doing this shit?* I stood there with a confused look on my face.

"Are you serious, Sincere? Drugs? What the fuck is your problem?"

"Chill out, Keiks. It's just a little bit of nose candy. That's all, that's it," Sincere said, nonchalantly.

I didn't even want to go hard on him right then, but just that fast, he had killed my mood.

"Let's go back out there."

He wiped off his nose and walked out the door. I jogged to keep up with him.

We made it back to the area where everyone was hanging out, and just like that, we went back to acting like the *perfect couple*. Everyone was congratulating us and telling Sincere how proud they were. The whole time I was thinking to myself, *if you only knew*. I was disappointed with Sincere, but by the way I carried myself, no one had the slightest idea about the secrets that I was keeping.

* * *

WE MADE IT TO THE CLUB FOR THE AFTER PARTY, AND I WAS beyond tired. My heels were killing my feet, and my head was pounding. I had to play it off because there were so many eyes on me the whole time. It is crazy how many things can change within a few months. Before I was the life of the fucking party, trying to catch me a rich nigga to fuck on, taking pictures for the Gram, and a bunch of other things. Now, I just wanted to be at home in my bed, getting some much needed sleep.

I was quiet after witnessing Sincere doing drugs, and he was too high to notice that my mood had shifted. As soon as I thought things were getting better, his ass always managed to do some shit. I was going to talk to him about it as soon as we made it home, but for now, I was going to let him enjoy his night.

The VIP section was lit. Everyone was poppin' bottles and I was sitting there sipping on water. My sober ass was well alert and peeping out the scene. All of Sincere's home-boys' were high as shit and had all types of groupie hoes in the VIP section. Some of them kept eyeing Sincere, and when Sincere thought I wasn't looking, he was eyeing them back. I kept shaking my head annoyed, but again I couldn't show that I was bothered. I would never give these bitches the satisfaction.

Everyone was having a good time, and I couldn't enjoy myself like I wanted to, but I sat my ass right down and waited until Sincere said it was time to go. I was looking around the club, and there were so many faces that I recognized. There were even niggas in there that I had fucked in the past, and whenever they would look my way, I turned away quickly.

"You alright, Keiks?" Sincere walked up to me and asked.

"Yeah, just a little tired, babe."

"Okay, we gon' leave soon, ma."

Sincere had this weird look in his eyes. It was like he was here physically, but mentally he was gone. It had to be the drugs, and I did not like it one bit. Two hours later, Sincere and I were walking out of the club. He was acting weird, but I tried to brush it off. I was feeling uneasy.

"Babe, do you want me to drive home?"

"Naw, I will drive," he insisted.

I let it go, but I still felt like I should've driven. He was drinking and doing drugs all night. We got in the car, and before I could even close the door, a pregnant woman pulled on the door.

"Sincere! Yo bitch ass is going to take care of yo fucking seed! You flaunting this bitch around and claiming her fucking unborn child. You are going to take care of this baby too!" the woman shouted.

I looked to see who the woman was, and after a minute, I recognized her. It was the same bottle girl from the club Sincere and I went to a while back. The same young girl who I saw sucking his dick in the room. *I thought Sincere told this bitch to get an abortion.* I just wanted to get home, and here I am about to get into some shit with this bitch.

Sincere's jaws clenched, and he was fuming. Luckily, there weren't that many people around when Sincere hopped out of the driver's seat and shoved her ass in the back seat before she could even yell for help. He looked around to make sure no one was around taking pictures or paying attention to us.

She was kicking and screaming in the backseat. I already had a headache, and this bitch is making it worse.

"Bitch, shut the fuck up! Your stupid ass should have never approached us in the first place. Now, if you don't stop fucking kicking my seat, I will come back there and beat the fuck outta you," I furiously spat.

"Bitch, fuck you!"

That was it. I took off my heels and climbed into the back seat and slapped her ass. She slapped me back. Thank God, my belly wasn't big yet then I wouldn't be able to fight her. I kicked her in the head. She tried to grab my leg, but I was too fast for her. I punched her in the mouth and blood squirted out all over Sincere's seat.

"Argh! You knocked out my tooth, bitch!" She held her mouth.

I looked at Sincere and he was just driving, not saying a word. He had two pregnant women fighting like animals, and he's driving like nothing is going on.

The young girl stopped fighting and cried. I got back into the passenger seat and was curious to find out where Sincere was driving to. We already drove past the exit to go home, so I knew he wasn't going there. He finally grabbed his phone and texted someone. I tried to see who he was texting, but he turned the phone so that I couldn't see.

Fifteen minutes later, the young chick was still crying in the backseat and blood was everywhere. Sincere pulled into a parking lot and there were two black trucks parked in front of a warehouse. *What the fuck are we doing here? He better not be doing no stupid shit.*

Sincere spoke. "Keiks, wait in here."

I nodded, but I was scared shitless.

He got out of the car and walked around to the back door and pulled out the young girl.

"Put me down, Sincere! I fucking hate your crazy ass!" she shouted out.

"Bitch, if you don't stop talking I'm gonna snap your fucking neck," he told her.

She probably knew that Sincere would do it, so she got quiet. He threw her over his shoulder and walked into the warehouse. I wanted to see what was about to happen inside, so I got out of the car and took my nosey ass to the door. I checked to see if it was unlocked and it was. I didn't see or hear anyone when I walked in, so I continued walking around until I heard movement upstairs. I slowly walked up the stairs and my eyes landed right on the young girl strapped to a bed. I stood to the side to avoid being seen.

She looked like she was sleeping, and in the corner a White man in a lab coat was setting up tools next to the bed. I looked to see where Sincere was, and I didn't see him in the room. My heart was thumping so fast, and I was starting to shake.

The man in the lab coat walked over to her with a knife in his hand. Slowly he cut open her stomach deep enough to pull out her tiny, underdeveloped, baby. I covered my mouth fast to stop myself from screaming. I was trauma-tized. I could not understand how Sincere could allow this to happen. As much as I wanted to fuck that girl up, I wouldn't even wish what I was seeing on my worst enemy.

"Didn't I tell yo stupid ass to wait in the fucking car," Sincere calmly said.

He was too calm, which scared me even more. I was caught, and I needed to find a way out of this quick before he flipped out on me.

The White man in the lab coat looked at the door wide-eyed. He rushed to close the door right before Sincere grabbed me by the hair.

"Ouch, Sincere! You're hurting me!"

"This is what happens to nosey muthafuckas."

He threw me across the room then walked toward me and punched me in my eye. I immediately felt my eye swelling up.

"Sincere, how could you do this to that girl? Her poor baby!" I cried while holding my belly.

He didn't say a word, he just stared down at me with his fists balled up.

"Sincere, man, come on. Don't do ya girl like that," I heard Jaylanni's voice before I saw his face.

Sincere didn't say anything, he just walked away toward the room where the young girl was. Jaylanni walked over to me and helped me up.

"Come on, Keiko, let me walk you back to the car."

I couldn't even say anything, I just cried. Before we could make it out of the front door, I heard Sincere running down the stairs.

"Fuck! Jay, man! We need to get out of here, quick! She's fucking dead! Sincere looked scared, and just that fast, he had sobered up.

"Damn, Sincere! Fuck, man!" Jaylanni angrily yelled.

Sincere grabbed me out of Jaylanni's grip and pulled

me toward the car. Jaylanni ran to one of the black trucks and drove off. As we were driving out the parking lot, I looked back at the warehouse and the White man was running toward the other truck with blood all over his lab coat.

I stared out of the window as the tears poured down my face. My life was turning into a fucking nightmare.

CHAPTER 20

$\mathcal{S}$incere sped away from the crime scene. I was panicking and shaking bad. I looked at the man I had grown to love, and I couldn't fathom how we'd gotten to this point. My rich famous rap star boyfriend is a crazy, cheating, woman beater, maniac. The world idolize him, fans love him to death, women would do anything to get a piece of him, and here I am, starting to wish that I was anywhere in the world but here.

Sincere pulled out his phone and dialed a number, "Yo, I need the clean-up crew at the spot, ASAP!"

I looked at him. *Was this something that he's done before? What did I get myself into?*

"Keiks, you better not ever repeat this shit to no one… Ever!" he warned.

"Okay."

We made it home, and I ran straight to the bathroom. I got into the shower and just stood there letting the water run down my face and body. The water along with my tears flowed down the drain. Right there in the shower, I asked

God to forgive me for all of my sins and the pain that I'd caused in the lives of the people who I loved or cared about. I finally understand why Siana was upset, and I was so sorry. I was sorry for leaving Samir hanging. I was sorry for sleeping with Joe. I was sorry for not dragging Stacks-Mami off the stage at the swinger's club. I was even sorry for setting up Melo. I did my dirt and now karma was kicking my ass.

I felt a lot of fluid between my legs, and when I looked down there was so much blood.

"Sincere!" I shouted hoping that he would hear me.

My body trembled and the blood continued to pour down my legs. Sincere ran up to the shower door and looked down.

"Keiko! What the fuck happened?" Sincere was petrified.

"Plee... aassee, get... help," my voice cracked.

Sincere ran out of the bathroom. I heard him calling the doctor. He came back to the bathroom, got in the shower with all of his clothes on, and held me.

* * *

The doctor informed Sincere and me that we had miscarried. Sincere dropped to his knees and cried out. I had never seen him this devastated. All of the stress, the fighting, and Sincere throwing me around had led to me losing my baby. Now, he was here crying when he was the muthafuckin' cause of all of this.

Sincere was supposed to go on tour soon, and I couldn't wait for him to leave. I needed some space; I was losing my fucking mind. I wanted to heal in peace without his bullshit. He went from having two babies on the way to having none. A night that was supposed to be special for him ended tragically, and there was no one that I could talk to about it. I no longer wanted to think about the pain that I had endured. I just wanted to escape it all. I took some sleeping meds and dozed off.

* * *

I FELL INTO A DEEP DEPRESSION AND HAD COMPLETELY LOST myself. I no longer cared about social media, fame, money, or the glamorous life. That shit wasn't worth the abuse or the stress. I was ready to claim my life back, without Sincere in it.

"Hey Sincere, we need to talk."

I walked into the arcade while Sincere played games with his boys.

"Not right now, Keiko. I'm busy," he brushed me off.

"No, it needs to happen right now."

Sincere paused and looked me up and down. "Y'all hear this shit? She came down here, demanding shit. Get out of my face, Keiks," Sincere and his boys laughed.

I was embarrassed as fuck. I turned around to walk out of the arcade, and Sincere walked in front of me and stopped me. "Matter-of-fact, stay, Keiko. You brought ya ass down here in these little ass shorts and tank top. You tryna flaunt *my* shit for my homeboys', Keiko?" Sincere asked, looking at me crazy.

"Sincere, please. I'm about to go back upstairs."

I tried to walk around him but he blocked the doorway. I looked back and all four of his homeboys' were staring. I rolled my eyes at them and looked at Sincere.

"Sincere, stop playing. Let me get out of here and I'll talk to you later."

"Y'all since my bitch likes to walk around half naked around my homeboys', I'ma let y'all get a little treat today," Sincere said with an evil smile.

My heart raced. I didn't know what Sincere had planned. I know he was not about to let his homeboys' have sex with me. I just knew he was not that crazy. I tried to run out of the arcade, but Sincere pulled me back in.

"I'ma let y'all get some of this fire head from my bitch."

"Sincere, fuck no! Are you crazy? No fucking way!" I retorted.

"I'm a little crazy, Keiks, but shit, you already knew that though. Go ahead, suck my boys up."

His thirsty ass homeboys' pulled out their dicks right away. I tried to fight back and run to the door again, but Sincere put me in a chokehold and brought me back in front of his boys. He pushed me down to my knees and one by one, the man that I once loved so deeply made me suck each one of his homeboys' dicks. I was humiliated. I felt disgusted and nasty. Once upon a time, I would've been down for some freaky shit like this, but not anymore. I didn't expect for a man who claimed that he loved me to do something like this. I realized at this moment that I needed to find a way to leave Sincere.

CHAPTER 21

I stayed in bed for days. I didn't even get up to wash my ass. Sincere left the house after he made me do that foul shit with his homeboys', and I haven't seen him since. I couldn't believe my life had ended up like this. Crazy part is, I have my own fucking money, but I am used to spending Sincere's money.

My notifications were going crazy, so I finally looked at my phone to see what was going on. I cringed when I saw a photo of Sincere and me on the night of the Hip Hop Awards. Sincere had posted the picture, and underneath the caption read, *Just me and my girlfriend. I love her life. We are sorry to inform you all that we have lost our baby. I'm breaking down, but I know we will get through these tough times. I love you, Keiko.*

This nigga had lost his rabbit ass mind. How could he act like he cared so much, even though he had me sucking up his homeboys' just a few days ago? I was starting to hate his guts, and it was time for my ass to leave him for good. Thousands of people were sending their condolences and leaving sweet messages. Some were even telling me that I was lucky to have such an amazing man by my side. *Yeah, right.*

I got out of bed and smelling my own body funk made my nose turn up. I turned on the faucet to run myself a hot bubble bath. I eased myself into the tub, put my head back and closed my eyes. I didn't even realize I fell asleep until I heard someone moving around in the bedroom. *Fuck. This nigga is back.*

I jumped out of the tub, dried my skin and threw on my Versace robe. I walked into the room and a light-skinned woman was sitting on my bed.

"Who are you?" I frowned.

"Ask Sincere," she said with an attitude.

Sincere walked into the room with a big smile on his face. I shot him a look, and he walked over to me.

"Hey Keiks, you haven't seen me in days, and this is the welcome that I get?" he asked, playfully.

I didn't even have the strength to respond. I brushed past him and walked out of the room. I didn't have time for this bullshit. Sincere was right on my tail.

"Bring that ass back here now! I brought Leela back to the house so we can have a little fun, baby," Sincere stood in front of me.

"Sincere, I'm done. I'm packing up my shit and leaving you. I can't do this shit anymore," I told him.

The smile on his face faded away quickly. "You are not going anywhere. You belong to me, and you'll leave when I tell you to leave."

I quickly jogged to our walk-in closet and grabbed my clothes off of the rack. Sincere walked into the closet and grabbed my hands.

"Let me go right now, Sincere. That bitch can have you because I don't want yo ass!"

"Leave me and I'll kill you, Keiko," he said with a deep dark twinkle in his eyes.

I paused. I knew what he was capable of and I wasn't ready to leave the world yet. I looked at him with hatred in my eyes.

"Yeah, I thought so. Now, take ya ass back in that room and go sit on the lounge chair," he demanded.

I followed his command. I was so mad that I didn't take the time to leave while he wasn't here.

I walked back into our bedroom and the bitch was on our bed naked. I looked at her, and if looks could kill, she would be dead right now. I sat in the chair and in walked Sincere acting cocky as ever. He removed his clothes, but not before pulling a condom out of his pocket.

The woman was smiling and looking at Sincere passionately. I bet she was feeling like she was *that bitch* because the famous Sincere had brought her back to his mansion.

His dick was standing at attention, and while he got ready to fuck this chick, I couldn't control my thoughts of cutting off his fucking penis and shoving it up his ass. The same dick that I once loved and craved so much was now something that I despised.

Sincere picked up a little bag off the floor and handed it to her. She opened the bag and poured some white powder on his hard dick. She squatted down and snorted the powder right off his dick. Then she got up and bent over on the bed that I shared with Sincere. He slowly slid his dick right in her pussy. They both looked high and acted like they were on a different planet while they fucked all over our bed. This bitch was cumming everywhere and screaming for dear life as Sincere pounded the fuck out of her pussy. I couldn't take it anymore. I got up, and Sincere gave me a look that made me sit my ass right back down. The woman looked at me and smirked.

I looked at her and felt remorse. I felt like I was staring my old self right in the eyes. She thought she was winning, but she had no idea what this life was really about. Unlike me, this woman was probably broke and trying to come up. I was mad because I had my own money and still wanted to be greedy by spending another man's money; now, I was paying the price. Whoever said the grass ain't always greener on the other side, was absolutely stating facts. I needed to find a way to get out of this situation before I ended up hurt, or dead.

* * *

THE NEXT FEW WEEKS SINCERE STAYED AT HOME TO WATCH me 24/7. His trifling ass had a different bitch in our bed every single night and made me change the sheets after he was done fucking them. Sometimes he would fuck me right before he fucked the next bitch. Sex didn't even feel the same with him anymore. I felt no pleasure whatsoever. He had his way with me and threw me to the side like a rag doll when he was done. I was afraid of Sincere; he would kill me if I tried anything. The more I stayed in this mansion that had become my cage, the more I hated it, but I hated Sincere even more.

"Keiks, baby, come down to the bowling alley right quick," Sincere said over the intercom that was installed in every room.

I was sitting in the movie theater room minding my business, and he just had to disturb my peace. I slowly got up to go into the bowling alley that is built inside of his mansion.

He noticed me at the door. "Babe, come take a picture with me right quick. We haven't taken a picture for the Gram in a while."

I was in no mood to take pictures with this nigga, and it showed on my face.

"Stop looking stupid and come over here. Make sure yo ass look happy as fuck to be standing here next to me in this picture too."

Sincere grabbed my hand and put it around his waist, and he put his arm around me. With the other hand, he held the phone. He made sure that I was smiling in every photo, then he posted them.

I was over doing all this fake shit for the Gram. People were eating this shit up. These people were so obsessed with celebrities and seeing all the money, traveling pictures, designer things, and all the luxury shit that they didn't even know what secrets were hidden behind every photo. I was addicted to social media before meeting Sincere. He changed my life completely, and it wasn't for the better.

The caption he put for our photos read, "*King and Queen Shit.*" The disrespect, he was a fucking fraud. The likes and reposts went up. Fans were going wild. In the comments some said they wished that they could have what Sincere and I have, some said we are what relationship goals look like, others said we look so in love, and many said we are the best couple in the industry. I threw up in my mutha-fuckin' mouth reading those comments.

I looked at the gossip websites and they had pictures of us all over. They were praising our *perfect relationship*. These people had no idea what was going on and it made me sick to my stomach knowing that I had young girls looking up to me, wanting to be in my shoes. I prayed for those young girls, and I hoped that they'd never have to go through this nightmare that I now called my life.

An article titled, *Young Entrepreneur,* stood out to me, because the man in a photo standing next to a woman looked familiar. I clicked on the link and it took me to another website with more photos of the man. Samir was smiling, exposing his beautiful deep dimples while posing in a navy blue suit. I read the entire article, and when I was done, the phone was soaked with my tears. The man who I looked down on for working a 9-5 had started his own garbage truck company and was already making seven figures. He talked about investing, ownership, and growing his Black-Owned business. What broke my heart the most was seeing the pregnant woman who stood beside him as he held her belly. I was torn. Samir was probably the man who I should've been with, but I was too busy chasing the glamorous life to notice that I was missing out on a great man. It could've been me in those photos, but I didn't value this man or take the time to give him a chance. I may have missed out on a real King, and it shows. Now, I was stuck with a crazy ass, filthy rich rapper who often beats my ass to a pulp and fucks around like pussy is going out of style. He had all the money in the world, but that didn't mean shit to me anymore.

I learned that money don't mean shit when your soul is ugly. All of these lost souls are running around in designer clothes, ice drippin' all over their bodies, driving fancy cars, living in mansions, traveling all over the world, and have an abundance of money, but deep down inside, they feel empty. Many experience mental issues that aren't visible because they learn how to filter and mask them in front of the world. This is me. All of this shit was no longer worth it to me.

CHAPTER 22

*S*incere was getting ready to go away for two months on tour, and I was excited for him to leave. I am going to take this opportunity to finally leave him. I was scared like a muthafucka, but I couldn't live this fake happy life anymore. I didn't know how I was going to do it, but I was going to come up with a plan. I thought about exposing his ass, but that would come with too much negativity that I cannot deal with, plus no one would believe me.

"Keiks, pack your shit you're coming with me on tour," Sincere demanded.

"Sincere, why can't I stay here? I still don't feel comfortable traveling around after the miscarriage," I lied, trying to come up with an excuse.

"The miscarriage was a while ago; you must be healed already because I've been deep guttin' that pussy," Sincere laughed.

I wanted to punch him so bad, but I had to keep it together if I wanted my plan to work.

"I haven't healed emotionally and mentally, babe. I'm still hurt that we lost our baby."

Sincere stared at me trying to determine my sincerity.

"If I leave your ass here, you better not try no shit, because when I come back, you will have to pay the consequences. You hear me, Keiko?"

"Of course, I won't try anything, bae. I'll be right here waiting for you to come back home to me," I was throwing it on thick, trying to talk him into trusting me.

"You can stay, but I'm gonna have one of my boys stay here to watch you," Sincere said and walked out of our bedroom.

Fuck, I didn't need one of his goons keeping tabs on me. I needed to get out of here and get as far away as possible from him. In my mind, our relationship was over. In his mind, we were still together. Playing these different roles—the *it* couple in the spotlight and submissive woman behind closed doors—was starting to take a toll on my mental. I was emotionally, physically, and mentally exhausted.

* * *

"COME GIVE ME SOME PUSSY BEFORE I LEAVE, KEIKS," Sincere kissed me.

I did not want his dirty dick inside of me, but I couldn't let him know that. I couldn't risk an ass beating.

"Okay, daddy," I rolled my eyes when he wasn't looking.

"Let me taste this sweet pussy first."

Sincere pulled off my panties aggressively. His tongue went right inside my pussy hole, and he tongue fucked me. I think he was enjoying it more than I was. His focus then shifted to my clit, and he licked it. As much as I didn't want to, it started to feel good. I fucked his face with so much force, until my juices came creeping out of my pussy.

Sincere got up, and his dick was ready to enter me. He stuffed my hole and stroked my pussy.

"I'm gonna miss you, baby. Daddy gon' hurry and come back to you, okay?" Sincere said, passionately.

"Okay, daddy. I'm gonna miss you too."

As Sincere's dick went in and out of my hole, I thought about all of those bitches he had fucked in front of me, and I was seething. His dick was poison.

I was so caught up in my thoughts, I didn't even feel Sincere's cum filling up my pussy. He got off of me and went into the bathroom. I watched him as he washed off his dick, brushed his teeth, got dressed, and sprayed his YSL Cologne all over himself.

He walked back to me and slid his tongue inside of my mouth. I almost bit down on his shit, but again I had to remember to play nice for now. I kissed him back.

"I love you, ma. I'ma be checkin' on you. I might fly you out wherever I'm at."

I sure hope and pray that he doesn't fly me out anywhere. I do not want to ever be in his presence after today.

"Alright, babe."

He was leaving and his boy who was going to keep an eye on me wasn't here yet, so I thought that maybe Sincere had forgotten and was going to leave me at the mansion alone.

Ding Dong! Ding Dong!

Fuck, so much for wishful thinking, the sound of the doorbell interrupted my thoughts.

"Oh, I forgot to tell you that Jaylanni is gonna stay here

with you, so don't try no shit because he's just as crazy as me."

Sincere gave me a peck and went to open the door.

I looked toward the door, and Jaylanni stood there with two suitcases. *Lawd, I hope I don't have to deal with a Sincere number two.*

Sincere gave Jaylanni dap before he turned around and blew me a kiss. His luxury tour bus was parked outside the mansion. Someone came to the door to grab all ten of his bags, and Sincere followed right behind.

I felt a sense of relief, like I could breathe until Jaylanni closed the front door.

"Alright Keiko, Sincere told me to lock you up in the secret room."

Secret room? My heart skipped a beat, *no no this cannot be happening.* He walked toward me, and I sprinted to the front door and tried to open it when I realized that Sincere must have secretly had the locks changed while we were having sex because I didn't notice this earlier. The only way that I could get out was if I had a key. I looked at Jaylanni and he was staring at me. The tears started to roll down my cheeks.

CHAPTER 23

*J*aylanni escorted me into the movie theater room, and I kept wondering why the fuck we were walking in here. I looked around trying to find something that I can use to protect myself, but I was out of luck. Sincere's sneaky ass had gotten rid of everything. Beads of sweat formed on my skin as I silently prayed to God. I prayed that He would answer my prayer and help me get out of this situation.

Jaylanni was quiet and focused on the task. He walked toward the black rug that Sincere had in the room. I always felt like the rug didn't quite fit in the theater room, but I never asked any questions. He knelt down and began rolling up the rug. I watched him closely. When the rug was finally rolled up, it revealed a door with a lock. Jaylanni looked at me, and I quickly looked away. I heard him punch in a code and the door opened up. *What the fuck is this?*

"Come over here, Keiko."

I slowly walked over to Jaylanni and tried to get a sneak peek of what was on the other side of this door. Stairs were leading down into a dark tunnel. Jaylanni grabbed my arm and led me down the stairs. At this point, I wasn't even going to fight back fearing what he would do to me if I did.

Once we made it to the bottom of the stairs, Jaylanni turned on a light switch and I stood there stuck looking at what was in front of me. This is the creepiest shit I'd ever seen in my life.

This crazy ass nigga had a secret dungeon built into his mansion. All of the time I'd spent in the theater room, and I had no idea that this was even here. It made me wonder what else Sincere was hiding. There were about four cages, and each cage had black snakes slithering around.

"Jaylanni! Please! I gotta get the fuck outta here!" my voice trembled.

"Keiko, do you see this shit? This is where Sincere wants me to leave you," he paused. Jaylanni sighed and then continued. "I can't do this shit, it don't fucking sit right with me at all."

My heart was crushed. This is what Sincere thought of me. He was willing to fucking torture me with snakes. He knew how much I feared snakes and this is how he was going to punish me. I looked at the snakes and shivered. I needed to get out of this creepy ass dungeon right away.

"Jaylanni, can we please talk upstairs. I can't stay in this room any longer."

He contemplated for a while before he helped me climb up the stairs back to the top. We were back in the movie theater room, and I sat in the recliner seat, relieved that Jaylanni had the heart to let me come back upstairs. My mind was racing a mile a minute.

"How could he do this, Jaylanni? Is this the first time he's done some shit like this?"

"Honestly, I don't know what goes through his mind at

times. He would probably try to off me if he knew that I wasn't going along with one of his plans right now, but I can't do this to you, Keiko. I don't know what I'm going to tell him when he calls, but that's something I'll have to figure out," Jaylanni said in a gentle tone.

He looked like he had a million things running through his mind too. We sat there in silence for what seemed like an eternity.

"That night at the warehouse when that pregnant girl died... it did something to me and that's when I realized I was done. The world sees a talented, wealthy man, but behind all the glitz and glamour lives a dark soul."

"I can't do this shit anymore. I gotta get out of this mansion and go somewhere far away, Jaylanni, but I know if he finds me, he will kill me."

"He'll be gone for two months, so you can take this time to figure something out. In the meantime, you gotta stay here. You don't want him to get suspicious because there's no telling what he would do next."

I thought about what Jaylanni said for a minute. Lord knows that I wanted to get as far away from this place as possible, but I would have to play along with Sincere's evilness just to save myself.

"Alright, I'll do it, Jaylanni. What is the plan?"

"Whenever he calls me, I'll tell him that you're in the dungeon. When he asks to FaceTime you, we'll have to act like you've been down in the dungeon the whole time. Got it?"

As much as I wanted to run away, this is something that we have to do for now.

"Okay, got it. Jaylanni?"

"Yeah, Keiko... what's up?"

"Thank you. I know you didn't have to do this with

Sincere being your right-hand man and all, but I really appreciate it."

I was so serious. I just knew that when Jaylanni arrived at the house, I was going to have to deal with another psycho, but he proved me wrong.

I silently said a thank you prayer to God before I walked out of the theater room. Jaylanni stayed behind to close the door that led to the dungeon.

* * *

DAYS WENT BY, AND SINCERE HAD YET TO CALL. I WASN'T complaining, but I was wracking my brain trying to come up with an escape plan.

Jaylanni was actually making my situation bearable. Getting to know Jaylanni was something that I wasn't expecting at all. He was a sweetheart, and I would have never known. Jaylanni and Sincere were total opposites.

Jaylanni stayed busy watching ESPN, and I spent my time thinking about life and finding ways to leave this mansion for good. I missed my freedom so much, and even though I had more money than I could handle, I missed making my own money.

I wasn't even on social media much these days. I signed on just to be nosey and signed right back off. There were a bunch of new big booty, big titty females becoming social media influencers and they were coming up by fucking with these rich niggas. It wasn't so long ago that I was in their shoes too, and now, everything seemed so foreign to me. I stared at photos of all of the new Insta-Baddies and wondered how many of them were faking it for the Gram.

I was getting ready to sign off IG when a photo of Sincere popped up on the screen. It was a picture of him on stage at one of his performances. The internet was going crazy over him. His concerts were all sold out, fans were camping out just to get a chance to meet Sincere for a few seconds, and groupies were following him to every show trying to be the lucky girl of the night. And here I was, staring at the photo lost in my own thoughts, wishing that I had never met him.

"Aye, you good, Keiko?"

I jumped. I didn't even hear him come into the kitchen.

"Yeah, I'm alright."

"Do you want to cook breakfast, or should I? You know I got skills," he chuckled.

I grinned, he was right. I had learned so much about Jaylanni in just a few days. He was an excellent cook, and I would pack on some pounds if I didn't stop eating up everything that he cooked. I learned that he was raised by a single father after his mother ran away with his father's cousin. His dad worked his ass off to make sure that Jaylanni never wanted for anything. He opened up to me, and it was only right that I open up about my childhood as well. We also talked about our first impressions of each other. He thought that I was just some hoe. I mean, he wasn't wrong, but in the beginning, I really did care about Sincere. He thought that I would be just another fling for Sincere. I told him that I thought he was Sincere's, *yes man*, because he always did everything that Sincere told him to do. After our deep conversation, I felt like we both viewed each other in a whole new light.

"It's cool, I'll cook." I flashed a broad smile.

"Alright now, don't try to kill a nigga," he laughed and gave me a serious look.

I quickly looked away and when I glanced back at Jaylanni, he was still staring at me. I blushed as I tried to ignore the look that I'd seen from men a million times. Before this, I had never looked at him in this way; he is Sincere's friend so that was off-limits. Now, staring back at him, I'm realizing how handsome he is. He's brown-skinned with dark, soul-piercing eyes, long neat dreads, muscular, and about six-two.

I needed to distract myself quickly from the tingle between my legs that I hadn't felt in a while. It was not the time, nor the place for that. Jaylanni sat in the kitchen on the barstool and he must have been having thoughts too because he quickly pulled out his phone as a distraction and looked through it. I decided to make a vegetarian omelet for us and some freshly squeezed orange juice. As I cooked, my mind was still all over the place. So many emotions filled my body, and I needed to get out of the house for some fresh air.

"Do you think after we're done eating, we can get out of the house for a little bit? I could really use some fresh air."

"Yeah, no problem. I'll drive."

I was so excited to get out of the house that I damn near swallowed my whole omelet and gulped down my orange juice.

"Damn, Keiko, your throat okay?" He looked over at me.

"Ha-ha! Shit, I was just trying to finish, so that we can get going," I laughed.

"I thought I was gon' have to rush your ass to the hospital the way you just swallowed that shit whole," he joked.

I was in tears from laughing so hard. Another thing that Jaylanni did the past few days was make me laugh. I couldn't remember the last time I'd had a good laugh, and it felt good after all of the things that I'd been through lately.

Jaylanni finished eating while I went to shower and get ready.

* * *

JAYLANNI DROVE TO MALIBU, AND I WAS ENJOYING THE VIEW and fresh air. I closed my eyes and enjoyed the breeze hitting my face. I felt liberated, and I wanted this feeling to last forever. Jaylanni sat quietly and allowed me to have my moment.

"Jay, can you please do me two huge favors?"

"Waddup?" He looked away from the road briefly to give me his attention.

"Can you please take me to the cemetery and then to my friend's house after?" I eagerly waited for his response.

"I got you. Just tell me where to go."

I smiled. "Thank you."

I turned on my GPS, and we were on our way to the cemetery. I was overwhelmed with emotions. I don't know what came over me, but I knew that these were things that I needed to do. It was now or never.

We pulled into the cemetery, and I could no longer hold back the tears. Jaylanni parked and looked at me. He gently rubbed my hands, but he didn't say anything. I know he didn't know what the fuck was going on, and I was in no mood to explain. I was happy that he allowed me to go through my shit without disturbing me.

I went to visit StacksMami's grave and broke down right there above her grave. She was so full of life and always happy. Her death broke my heart all over again. I sat there and thought about her crazy *spa party*, and her wild ass taking me to the swinger's club just to help me take my mind off of getting exposed by Melo.

I dusted off her headstone with my jacket and said a prayer. I stood there for a minute just staring at her headstone. I still couldn't believe her lifeless body was buried here. I couldn't handle being here any longer. I blew a kiss to her grave before walking back to the truck where Jaylanni waited for me.

He was just ending a call when I entered the truck.

I looked at him through red and swollen eyes.

"Is everything okay?"

"Yeah, are you okay?"

"I'm hanging in there." I was really trying to stay sane through all the madness.

"If you need to talk, I'm here."

"Thanks, Jay."

Next stop, I was going to pull up on Siana. My nerves were getting the best of me as we drove on the highway to Siana's house. I didn't know how she would react or what to expect.

We pulled up to her block and parked in front of her house. I noticed two brand new Benz in her driveway. I got out of the truck and walked to the front door. Before pressing the doorbell, I quickly inhaled then exhaled to calm myself down. I stepped to the side and pressed the doorbell.

"I'm coming!" I heard Siana's voice yell from inside.

The door opened and Siana stood there glowing in a dress with a big belly that looked like she was going to pop soon. I tried to stop the tears, but it was too late. My best friend, my sis was pregnant, and I had missed out.

Siana's eyes got watery as soon as our eyes connected,

and she came close to me to give me a hug. *This is what I've been missing, my best friend... my sis.*

"Come in, Kei," Siana held the door open wide enough for me to get in.

Her whole place was remodeled, looking like a brand-new home. There were photos all around and as I looked closer, I noticed that they were wedding pictures. She had married Zay, *wow.* Siana was married, and it dawned on me that I had missed out on that too. I kept looking at the pictures and my eyes landed on pictures of Siana and myself. I turned around and looked at her. I couldn't believe that she put up pictures of us even though I did her dirty.

Siana read my mind.

"Kei'na, I love you. You will forever be my family. I forgive you. After I had time to reflect on the situation, I know that deep down you did not mean any harm. I blocked you because I saw the path you were on, and I knew that I couldn't tell you anything or stop you. I decided to step back and allow you to learn on your own. I couldn't sit back and watch you destroy yourself. I knew that you would be coming here to see me when the time was right."

"Sis... I'm so sorry. I'm so sorry. I'm so sorry. I love you and I've missed you so much," I cried my eyes out.

"I've been seeing you all over the news, gossip sites, magazines, and TV with Sincere. Kei, you are not happy, every photo that you take with him I see the pain in your eyes behind those fake smiles."

Siana read me like a book. I looked down, too damn ashamed to tell her that she was right, especially after seeing how happy she looked in the photos with her husband.

"Tell me what's going on, Kei'na. Is he hurting you?" she asked with sadness in her tone.

I kept looking down until I could no longer hide the truth. This is the first time that I was going to tell someone all of the secrets I was keeping to myself. I told Siana every single thing, and I didn't leave anything out.

Siana and I were both in tears when I was done.

"What's going on? Babe, are you okay?" Zay walked in rubbing his eyes like he just woke up from a nap. He realized that I was sitting there and looked at Siana then back at me.

Before he could say a word, I got off of the couch and walked over to him leaving some distance between us.

"Zay, I really want to apologize for my behavior that day at the pool party. That was very unacceptable and disrespectful. Please forgive me."

I was really sorry for my actions in the past.

"Kei'na, we have already forgiven you. You are family."

He gave me a friendly hug and left us alone to finish talking. After that moment, I knew that my sis was in good hands, and that she had lucked up and married a good man. If only, I was so lucky.

I was so caught up in everything else, I didn't even congratulate Siana on her marriage and her unborn baby.

"Sis, congratulations on your marriage and this beautiful blessing growing inside your belly. What are you having?" I reached over and rubbed her belly.

"Thank you, Kei. I'm having a girl," she smiled and placed her hand on top of mine.

All of a sudden, Siana's smile went away and she gave me a serious look.

"You need to pack your shit and get as far away as you can from Sincere. He's going to hurt... or kill you if you stay, Kei. Please, I'm begging you. You are a Queen, and no Queen deserves that type of treatment. If a man can't cherish and respect you in every way possible, then he's not for you, sis. No money, designer shit, fancy cars, or mansion is worth you losing your life over. You have your own, and you've always held your own. He doesn't own you, so get your ass out of there. And if you feel like you can trust his boy, Jaylanni, then he shouldn't have a problem helping you. Even if you need Zay to help, he will be willing to do so. I love you Kei'na, and I don't want anything else to happen to you." Siana was crying hysterically.

I felt bad because I didn't want her crying, it wasn't good for her or the baby.

"I'm going to get going now, sis. Don't worry, I'm going to be gone before Sincere comes back to Cali. I love you so much. Please unblock me, sis, I will keep you posted." I got up to give her a hug.

"I will be checking on you, sis. I love you. Kei?"

"Yes?"

"Please be careful."

She had that serious look on her face again, and I definitely understood why. Siana knew me better than anyone else.

CHAPTER 24

*V*isiting the cemetery and seeing Siana did something to my soul. I finally felt like I have all of the courage that I need to leave. Jaylanni is going to help me or go back and tell Sincere. He's been a sweetheart thus far, and I doubted he would do anything to jeopardize our newfound friendship. Plus, he was well aware that his boy was a legit psycho.

"Jay, we have a few weeks left before Sincere gets back. I need to be gone by the time he steps foot back in Cali."

Looking up from his phone Jaylanni nodded, "I agree. We gon' get you away from here. Don't trip."

I stared at him, and I couldn't help but feel a way about Jaylanni. For days I'd been trying to fight the feeling, but I was starting to like him. He wasn't a superstar, and that was absolutely okay. He made his money by investing, as well as his other business ventures. For the first time in my life, I didn't care what a man have or didn't have. I know that I didn't fully know him yet, but I was liking the things that I did know.

Jay was nothing like Sincere, and that made me like him even more.

If Sincere knew that I was catching feelings for his right-hand man, he would probably kill us both and have someone else cover it up. Money really talks. I wasn't going to make a move on him, but if he ever made a move on me, I wouldn't stop him.

"If you want, you can stay at my place in the valley for a little while until I get things situated with him. Sincere would never look there," he said, interrupting my thoughts.

"That's so sweet of you, but I can't crash at your place like that. I think I'm going to rent another condo so that I can have a doorman for protection. I might look into hiring a bodyguard."

"Alright, if you insist. Let me know if you change your mind."

"I'm actually going to go look at a few places today."

"Do you need me to come with you?"

"No, I got it. I'll come back when I'm done to start packing up my things. I'm going to put everything in storage, so when it's time to dip, I can easily get my ass out of this fucking hellhole."

That was only part of the reason why I wanted to go alone. I still didn't trust anyone entirely, so I didn't want anyone to know where I was going to reside.

"I'm gonna go take a quick nap before I do anything because I barely slept last night."

I looked over at him, and he was undressing me with his eyes.

"Okay, I might do the same, then I gotta go handle a few things while you're gone."

"Alright."

I walked into the guest room where I'd been sleeping.

The room that I shared with Sincere was tainted with bad memories. He had all types of dried up pussy juice all over the bed that I once loved being in.

I removed my clothes and cozied up under the thick blanket. I couldn't fall asleep right away, so I did what I knew would help me fall asleep quickly. I moved my fingers down to my pussy and slowly rubbed my clit. It had been a while since I played with myself, and I had forgotten how good I could make myself feel. I closed my eyes and grinded my pussy all over my fingers. I sped up a little bit as my pussy juice coated my fingers.

My blanket slid down from the speed of my fingers rubbing my pussy. I opened my eyes to adjust the blanket back over my body, and my eyes met with Jaylanni's eyes. I quickly removed my fingers from my now soaking wet pussy and pulled the blanket over my naked body.

"Um... I'm sorry, Keiko. I was just checking on you. I thought you were sleeping," he said, his voice cracking.

"Jay, my bad. I couldn't fall asleep." I nervously looked away.

He stood there stuck for a minute staring at me, not knowing what to say. *Fuck it.* I stared back at him no longer hiding the fact that I was feeling him.

He moved closer to the bed and gently removed the covers from my body. I didn't stop him. The tip of his fingers slowly traced over my whole body, and he left goosebumps behind. The feeling was something new and I liked it. Then he bent down and placed his thick lips over mine. I parted my lips to allow his tongue entry into my mouth. Our tongues connected and intertwined. The passionate kiss that we shared had my fucking pussy screaming out.

Jay removed his white tee and guided my body toward

the edge of the bed. He opened my legs and stared down at my pussy.

"Whew! This pussy is wet-wet," he chuckled.

I giggled, "Yeah, she is."

He got down on his knees between my legs and dived right in. Jay's warm wet tongue ate me up like this is the meal he'd been waiting for his whole life. He sucked on my clit until I was shaking and holding on to the sheets for dear life. He licked up and down my slit not missing a spot. I had died and gone to ecstasy.

Jaylanni grabbed my hips and pulled my pussy closer to his mouth. I was gyrating my hips on his tongue like I was dancing to a reggae song. This shit was feeling so good, and it was much needed. There was only so much that my fingers could do, so I was happy that his tongue had replaced my fingers. I enjoyed the way Jay licked and sucked all over my pussy. He pushed my legs as far back as they could go and ate my ass. *Ooowee, and he eats ass too.* Jay held my ass and pussy wide open as his tongue went back and forth between the two. His fingers slid inside of my pussy hole and he finger fucked me. I was cumming all over the bed, his fingers, his lips, his tongue, and his chin.

"I'm cummin', Jay… I'm cummin'!" I shouted as I exploded. I was beyond exhausted.

He got up to wipe off his face, and I could see his dick poking out through his basketball shorts. *Yup, I need to feel that next.* I looked at him and licked my lips, then looked down at his dick, letting my eyes do the talking.

Jaylanni got the hint real quick. He pulled out his dick and held his long juicy looking dick in his hands. I leaned up and crawled over to where he stood and slid his dick into my mouth. Jay's dick was fat and long. *Hmmm… this is going to fill my pussy up real good.* It had been too long since I've had a bomb enjoyable dick and I was going to cherish every second of the deep dicking that was coming.

I sucked and jerked his dick. I made sure it hit the back of my throat every time. I played with the head with my tongue. I was spitting all over his dick and that drove him crazy.

"Awe, shit, Keiko!" he grunted.

I sucked even faster until his body tensed. Shortly after I felt his thick warm nut moving down my throat. I made sure I swallowed all of it, and nothing was left behind.

"Fuck!" Jay's legs were weak as he plopped down on the bed to catch his breath.

I was ready to feel him, but I allowed him to rest up before I bust this pussy open for him.

I didn't have to wait long at all. Jaylanni's dick shot right back up minutes later. *That's what the fuck I'm talking about.*

I laid on my back, legs spread, and my pussy ready for some action. We didn't even worry about protection. As his dick entered my wet hole, he tilted his head back, closed his eyes, and bit into his lip when he felt the inside of my pussy. Shit, I felt the same as his dick went inside me. The feeling shooting through my body was indescribable.

Jaylanni fucked me all over the guest room like he knew my body inside out. He was pounding me until we were both cumming again. When he didn't pull out, I did not even give a fuck. I must admit, I was dickmatized just that fast.

I wanted to go for another round, but we were both tired. Jay was already sleeping next to me, and I was right behind him. Before falling asleep, I thought about Sincere. He would flip if he ever found out about his boy dicking me down in his home. *Shit, oh well.* He didn't have a problem when he forced me to suck his other homies' dicks. So, fuck what he thought. However, I was happy that he left Jaylanni in-charge of *watching me*. This watchman was perfect. I smiled and drifted off to sleep.

* * *

"KEIKO, KEIKO!" JAYLANNI SHOOK ME OUT OF DEEP SLEEP.
   "Huh?"

"We gotta go down to the dungeon! Sincere just texted me saying he's gonna FaceTime after he gets off stage because he wants to see you." Jaylanni said with malice in his voice.

"Ugh, do I have to Jay?" I asked, rolling my eyes.

"Remember the plan, beautiful."

I dreadfully got out of the bed and threw on a t-shirt and sweats. I followed Jay to that creepy ass dungeon and almost died when a snake slithered across my feet.

Jay's phone started to ring alerting him that a FaceTime call was coming in.

"Yo," Jay answered dryly.

"Let me see that bitch!" Sincere yelled.

Jay pointed the camera at me, and I immediately went into actress mode. I acted like I had been locked up for days and suffering. Sincere looked at me with an evil smile painted on his face.

I wanted to curse his ass out so bad, but I had a role to play. I looked like I was a sad puppy.

"You enjoying my *secret room*, Keiks? You betta be taking good care of my lil' friends in there," he burst out in laughter.

Jay's jaw clenched and his fist rolled up, but I gave him a quick look to help calm him down. I really wanted to be petty and tell his ass that his friend had just got done beating up my pussy, but I held my tongue.

"I'll be home in two more weeks, and I gotta lil' surprise for you, Keiks. A'ight ma, I gotta go fuck this groupie bitch right quick. You know these bitches stay throwing the pussy." He hung up the call.

"I fucking hate him!" I screamed at the top of my lungs.

I dashed for the stairs, I hated being in this dungeon. Jay was right on my heels. When we got into the theater room, Jay held me in his arms.

"I'ma handle this, Keiko. Don't worry, okay?" Jay backed away from me far enough to look me in my eyes.

"Okay."

I would not be here to see no fucking surprise that Sincere thought he was going to give me. I would be long gone by then. I still couldn't believe that this is the same man that had me head over heels in love with him just a few months ago. He had put a damper in my mood, but I was not about to give that nigga the opportunity to ruin my life even more.

CHAPTER 25

I signed the lease for a beautiful condo, and the best part was the number of security officers all over the building. Everything was fully furnished and brand new. I wanted something a little roomier than my last condo since I would be spending most of my time inside anyway. There are four bedrooms and four bathrooms. Everything in the condo is modern, which is what I prefer.

I was feeling so good and excited to end this chapter with Sincere and move on with my life. I just hoped that he would move on after he found me gone. I also prayed that he didn't try to harm Jay for letting me *get away*.

My phone vibrated in my back pocket, and I pulled it out to see who was calling. Seeing Jaylanni's name on the screen gave me butterflies.

"Hey, Jay."

"Hey Keiko, is everything good with you?" He sounded like he was smiling.

"Yeah, I just got done signing the lease for my new place," I told him excitedly.

"Cool, cool. Congrats beautiful. When we get back, we'll pack up all of your things."

"Okay, see you soon." I ended the call and held my phone close to my heart. Jay was doing some *thangs* to me, and it wasn't all physical.

My phone vibrated again, and when I looked, it was Siana calling me. I quickly answered her call.

"Hey Si, you good?"

"I'm going into labor, Kei, I need you."

"Omg, sis! Text me the hospital address, and I'll be on my way."

My heart was beating so fast. I was nervous and happy for Siana.

I texted Jay to let him know where I was going and left my new condo in a hurry. My sis is going to be a mother, and I still couldn't believe it. Many things had changed for us in just a short time. I was lost in my thoughts on the way to the hospital.

* * *

I WAS HOLDING MY GOD-DAUGHTER, ZALIYA RAE, IN MY arms, and I was absolutely in love with her. Siana was in labor for twelve hours, and I gotta give it to her, she was a trooper. Zay was by her side the whole time supporting her. I felt the love between the two of them as I watched from the side. I couldn't help but think about my own life. I wondered if I would ever get to experience something so special in my life.

Zaliya was starting to get fussy because she was hungry. I gently placed her back into Siana's arms, so that she could breastfeed her precious baby girl.

I was exhausted, and I still needed to pack my things

with Jay. He had sent several messages checking on me, and at this point, I was starting to miss him.

"Si, I'm going to get out of here. Congratulations again, sis; you did an amazing job. And thank you for making me Zaliya's God mom." I was smiling from ear to ear.

"Thank you, Kei. I really appreciate you being here. It means so much to me."

"I got you and this beautiful baby always, Si."

"Did you find a place yet? Please tell me that you did," she said in a serious tone.

"Right before you called me, I had just finished signing my lease."

"I'm so happy to hear that. You already know what I'm about to say... please be careful, Kei. I love you."

She extended her free hand toward me, and I held onto it giving her a gentle squeeze. I gave her and Zaliya a kiss on the cheek and left the hospital.

* * *

WHEN I WALKED INTO SINCERE'S MANSION, A STRONG aroma hit me. I followed the scent into the kitchen and Jaylanni was throwing down listening to oldies. I leaned on the kitchen doorway and watched him. He didn't see or hear me.

"Hmm, hmm," I cleared my throat.

Jaylanni turned around and gave me a huge smile.

"Damn girl, how long have you been standing there?"

"Long enough to see you dancing around," I laughed.

He walked over to me and gave me a hug. Our bodies were practically connected as he held me close. We danced in the kitchen, and at that moment I decided I wanted to be with Jaylanni and didn't care about the consequences. I kissed him, and he anxiously kissed me back.

"Let me go shower. I've been running around all day." I pulled away from him.

"Okay baby, when you're done we'll eat shrimp pasta for dinner, and for dessert, I made banana pudding."

My stomach was growling non-stop, so I hurried off to get myself cleaned up. In the shower, I let the hot water beat against my skin as I thought about the man that was waiting for me downstairs. I wished that Jaylanni was the man that I had met first, but back then with the mindset I had, I probably wouldn't have even given him a chance.

I heard the door open, and Jaylanni walked in naked. *Damn, this nigga is looking good as fuck.* We looked at each other seductively and already knew what time it was. I was ready to feel his balls slapping against my pussy lips. I turned off the water because I didn't need us slipping and sliding in this shower or all of my pussy juices washing away. I need all of it to coat Jaylanni's dick. I need it to be wet and sticky icky.

Following my lead, Jay dried off my body, and when I was dry enough for him, he bent me over on the bathroom sink. He gripped and groped my ass, and then he ate my pussy from the back. I was drippin' wet when he was done.

I felt the tip of his dick playing with my pussy, and when I couldn't take it anymore, his dick slipped right inside of my wetness.

"Ahh, mhm Jay... fuck this pussy with that big dick," I moaned.

"You like this shit, baby?"

"Yes, daddy!" I hollered as cum gushed out of my pussy.

Seconds later, Jay's cum filled me up and dripped out of

me. We tried to catch our breath before he turned around to turn on the shower again.

We took a shower together, and Jay washed my whole body from head to toe. I returned the favor. *This is something that I can get used to.*

* * *

JAY AND I WERE CHILLIN' IN THE THEATER ROOM WATCHING reruns of *Living Single* when his phone chimed.

"It's that bitch ass nigga calling," Jay said, angrily.

He held the phone in his hand not wanting to answer.

"Baby, remember our plan," I reminded him.

"Yeah?" Jay said dryly.

"What's up with you, nigga? You straight?" Sincere asked, suspiciously.

"Yeah, man. I was taking a nap."

"Keiko ain't been acting up, right? How is she handling being locked up in the dungeon?"

I rolled my eyes. Jaylanni paused. "How do you expect someone to act while being locked up in a dungeon?" he snapped.

Fuck.

"Nigga, don't let me find out you getting fucking soft on me. Don't trip, I'll be home to handle that bitch myself. Make sho to leave her ass in there until I get there." Sincere ended the call.

"Fucking son of a bitch!" Jay yelled.

"Calm down, baby. Fuck that nigga."

I quickly tried to cease the tension that was building up in the room. I held Jaylanni until I felt him calming down in my arms. He pressed his lips against mine and hugged me tightly.

"I won't ever let that nigga hurt you again, Keiko. I know this is a weird situation, but I want you to be mine. I'll always protect you," he whispered in my ear.

"Nothing would make me happier than being yours, Jay." I kissed him passionately, hoping that he could feel how serious I am.

Jay picked me up and took me into one of the guest bedrooms and made love to me for the rest of the night. He exploded inside of my pussy, back-to-back.

I now had a real boyfriend. Technically, I had two boyfriends, but one didn't know that I had mentally checked out of the relationship a long time ago. Once I was far away from Sincere, it would just be Jaylanni and me.

CHAPTER 26

*J*ay helped me pack up all of my things. We loaded up all of my clothes, bags, and shoes into my truck, and the other larger items we piled into a moving truck that we rented. Those things were going into a storage unit.

I still wasn't sure if I wanted Jay to know where I was going to live yet, I was just so afraid of making the wrong move. I know that since we decided to take things to the next level, I needed to learn how to trust him, but for now, it was best to keep this information to myself for a little while longer.

It seemed like Jay understood how I felt even without me having to say anything. He didn't ask any questions or pressure me into telling him where my condo was located.

"Babe, after we drop these things off at your storage, we are going to stay at my place tonight. Sincere is coming back home in a couple of days, and we will not be here. All hell will break loose, but I will deal with that," he said, firmly.

I nodded my head. I was ready to put all of this behind me. Jay hopped in the rental moving truck, and I got into my truck. He was going to take care of putting my things into storage, and I was going to take all of my clothes, bags, and shoes to my condo. I told him that I was going to stop by Siana's house to visit her and the baby too. We agreed to meet back at the mansion later.

* * *

I PULLED INTO SIANA'S DRIVEWAY AND USED THE SPARE KEY that she gave me years ago to let myself into her house. I heard the baby cooing in the back of the house. I followed the sounds and it led me into her pink and gold nursery. Zaliya was the cutest baby ever. My heart melted when I looked at her. She was kicking and throwing little punches into the air with a smile on her face.

I still didn't see Siana, so I left the nursery and walked around the house searching for her. I walked into her bedroom, nothing. The last room to check was her master bathroom. I walked into the bathroom, and there my sis was deep throating her husband. Normally, I would've stood there and watched, but that was the old me. They were so caught up in getting their freak on that they didn't even hear me, so I quietly backed away from the door and went back to my God baby's room.

I was rocking Zaliya in the rocking chair, and we both were dozing off.

"Hey Kei, when did you get here?" Siana stood in front of me nervously.

I wanted to say, *long enough to see you giving head like a pro just like the way I taught you.* "Not that long. I came straight to the room to see Zaliya."

"Oh okay. How are you? Did you move yet? Is Jaylanni helping you? What is going on with you and him?" Siana was asking questions back-to-back.

"Dang, sis, ask me a hundred questions why don't you." We both burst out in laughter.

"Well to answer your questions. I'm doing much better now. All of my things are either in storage or in my condo. Jaylanni has been such a big help, you have no idea, sis. As far as Jaylanni and I…"

Siana impatiently waited for my answer. "Girl, tell me."

I chuckled, "He is amazingggggg!"

"I've never seen you all gushy over no man before. It is refreshing to see you like this. Jaylanni must be special."

"He is Si, but you know I'm taking my time after all that I've been through, and you know, with him being Sincere's friend and all." The mention of Sincere's name left a bitter taste in my mouth.

"Shit, it sounds like they will not be friends for much longer. Do not worry about all of that, just focus on making sure you're good first, sis."

"You're right, sis." I gave her a warm smile

All of a sudden, my stomach felt uneasy. I quickly got up from the rocking chair and handed Siana the baby. I rushed to her guest bathroom and barely made it to the toilet as all of the food that I had for breakfast came pouring out into the toilet.

"Kei! Are you okay?" Siana looked frightened.

I looked up at her, and I knew that I was looking crazy with vomit still on the sides of my lips.

"I don't know what's going on, Si. I must have eaten something bad this morning," I said, confused.

"Kei, I think you need to take a pregnancy test."

I hadn't even thought about being pregnant again until

that moment. I started to breathe heavily as a million thoughts were running through my mind.

Siana rushed off and came back a minute later with a glass of water and two pregnancy tests.

"Here, drink this water and take these tests. I still have some pregnancy tests from when I was pregnant." She handed me the water, tests, and closed the door.

I drank the water and unwrapped the first pregnancy test. I urinated on the stick and waited for the results. As the minutes passed, I was too afraid to look at the results. I slowly picked up the stick and looked at it.

OMG! Positive! I tore open the second pregnancy test and repeated the process again. Thank goodness I still had to pee, I had just enough urine left for the second pregnancy test. Again, I waited for the results.

"You okay in there, Kei?" Siana asked on the other side of the bathroom door.

"Uh yeah, give me a minute, Si. I'll be out shortly."

I looked at the results from the second test. There was a big fat positive again. I stood there frozen and panicking. I don't know whether Sincere or Jaylanni is the father.

CHAPTER 27

I had no idea how far along I was. I had sex with Sincere right before he left for his tour, and Jaylanni and I were fucking like jackrabbits since Sincere has been gone. I was in a serious dilemma and I didn't know what to do. I didn't want to keep this important information from Jaylanni; he needed to know.

I explained the situation to Siana, and she was very supportive.

"Kei, first thing first you need to book a doctor's appointment. Second, you must talk to Jaylanni and let him know what's going on."

"I will, sis. Actually, I'll use this app to book an appointment right now. Hopefully, I can get an appointment today before I meet up with Jaylanni, just so that I can know more information before I talk to him tonight."

"Besides all of that... I'm excited! I'm going to be an auntie!" Siana squealed.

I had to laugh at her silliness. She hugged me, then ran her hand across my flat stomach.

"You are going to be good Kei, believe it."

"I sure hope so, Si."

I had an appointment in the next two hours, so I left Siana's house to get a snack before my appointment.

* * *

"Ms. KONNERS, YOU ARE FOUR WEEKS PREGNANT. Congratulations!" the female doctor said, excitedly.

I sat on the hospital bed staring at the doctor, but my mind was far away. If I was four weeks pregnant that meant that Jay is the daddy. I was relieved that Sincere's seed was not growing inside me, but I was afraid of what Sincere would do when he finds out that I am carrying another man's baby and that man is his *friend*.

The doctor gave me a photo from my ultrasound, my prenatal pills, and a bunch of forms about my growing baby. God was giving me another chance, and this time I felt like I would be having a baby with the right man. I couldn't wait to get back to Sincere's house to see Jaylanni and let him know the good news.

* * *

JAYLANNI STILL HADN'T MADE IT BACK TO SINCERE'S mansion, so I waited in my truck until he arrived. I haven't been on social media in a long time, and it had been even longer since I'd posted a photo. I had an eerie feeling as I looked through my IG, something just didn't feel right to me.

As if right on cue, my notifications and messages started coming in. The same feeling that I had in the past when I was exposed came over me. I hesitantly clicked on the first notification.

Oh no, oh no, oh no… FUCK! There were two photos of me sucking Sincere's four friends' dicks the day he forced me to do it. *That sneaky fucking bastard!* He had set me up. He had a motive this whole fucking time, and I fell right into his trap. I was so humiliated. My mind went straight to Jaylanni. He would not want me after seeing this shit. I looked at Sincere's page and he had just posted a picture of himself throwing up the middle finger with stacks of money on his lap. The caption said, *never turn a hoe into a housewife, money over bitches*. This crazy nigga really acted like I secretly went behind his back and did this shit. People were leaving comments talking all kinds of shit about me. Some were telling him how bad they felt for him. It was a fucking pity party in his comment section, and these muthafuckas really had no idea that their *idol* was really the devil himself. I deactivated my IG and threw my phone on the passenger seat.

My phone started to ring, and I looked to see who was calling. Jaylanni. My heart raced. I answered the phone frantically.

"Jay, I can explain, baby."

"No need to, babe, I know what Sincere made you do," he said in a sad tone.

I was bawling into the phone, the tears were pouring out and weren't letting up.

"It's okay, baby. The world don't know what that nigga made you do, all they see is a picture, but they don't know the story behind that foul shit. Keiko, don't let that shit stop you from shining, baby. You'll get through this just like you've gotten through everything else in your life. Only difference is that this time, I'll be right by your side," he assured me.

After almost two months of getting to know Jaylanni, I was in love with him.

"Jay, I love you," I cried out.

"I love you too, Kei'na," he said using my government name.

My heart smiled. I genuinely loved this man who lifted my spirits more than anyone I have ever dated.

"I'm pulling into the driveway right behind you," he said.

I turned around and sure enough, my man was right behind me. I opened my door and ran into his arms. Jay held me close to him, and he didn't let go for a while.

"Let's go inside, babe. I gotta get my bags right quick before we go to my place."

I followed behind Jay into the mansion that I now despised so much. We went straight to the room where his bags were, and he threw the rest of his things into it. I looked around and it finally hit me that I would be leaving this big ass mansion forever. The mansion where Sincere tried to keep me locked up. I turned to look at Jay and he was already staring at me.

I walked over to him and wrapped my arms around his neck. We shared a kiss and not too long after, I felt his manhood poking through his jeans. I could feel the moistness in my panties. Jay stepped out of his jeans and boxer briefs, and I removed my shorts and panties. He gently pushed me onto the bed and spread my legs. Jay knew how much I loved getting head before getting the dick, so he aimed to please me. He lifted my shirt exposing my hard brown nipples. He popped my nipple into his mouth, and he showed love to my other nipple too. Then he kissed all over my body and his head moved down to his favorite place.

My clit was already poking out from my legs being spread so wide. He went straight to my clit and tongue kissed it.

"Mmnhm..." I moaned.

Jay was eating my pussy up and I was squirming all over the bed. The bed was turning into an ocean as much as I was creaming all over it.

Right before I was about to cum, Jay slipped his thick dick right into my wet pussy. He was pumping in and out, and I was tightening my pussy muscles every time he went inside. He was beating it up slow and then fast, he was giving me that bomb ghetto loving that I love so damn much.

"So, this is what the fuck you grimy muthafuckas been up to, and why yo bitch ass been talking crazy to me!" Sincere's voice echoed through the mansion.

Fuck! This nigga came back a day early. Jay's dick was so deep in my pussy, and I was so angry at Sincere for disturbing our fuck session.

Sincere looked from me to Jay emotionless. I didn't know what he was about to do, but I was not about to stick around to find out. I quickly put my panties and shorts back on, and when I looked at Jay he was putting on his clothes too.

"Sincere, you've been doing Keiko wrong, and I will no longer sit back while you continue to fucking ruin her life. From now on, stay the fuck away from my woman," Jaylanni ordered as he came over to me and placed his hand on my lower back.

We brushed past Sincere and he was still standing in the same position not saying a word.

"Babe, your bags," I whispered to Jay.

"Fuck those bags. Let's get out of here."

My adrenaline was so high, and all I wanted to do was safely make it out of this mansion alive with Jaylanni.

I was surprised that Sincere still hadn't chased us down. Maybe he was still in shock about what had just transpired.

"Follow me, baby," Jay said, calmly.

I jumped in my truck and Jay got in his car too. I was going to follow him to his house. I was happy that Jay had never told Sincere about his second home in Rancho Cucamonga because I know he would come after us.

Rat! Tat! Tat! Tat!

Sincere sprayed our vehicles, and my heart dropped to the floor before the world went dark.

CHAPTER 28

I woke up in the hospital, and my hands went right to my stomach. *My baby*! All I remember is Sincere shooting at us. *OMG, Jaylanni!* I tried to get up, but I was hooked up to so many machines. I was panicking. I needed to know that my baby and Jaylanni were okay.

"Nurse! Nurse! Somebody please, help me!" I yelled.

Two nurses ran into the room. "Ms. Konners, you're up!"

"Tell me that my baby and my man are okay!"

"Please calm down, Ms. Konners, so that we can talk to you," the elderly nurse told me.

I wanted to turn the fuck up in that hospital, but that wouldn't do any good. I stared at them and waited for them to tell me more.

"Your baby is doing well sweetheart, as for the gentleman... he's fighting for his life." she said.

"No!" I balled up into a fetal position and cried my eyes and heart out. I needed to see Jaylanni. He had to pull through. I didn't even tell him about his seed. I couldn't lose the love of my life.

"I'll take it from here Nurse Love, and Nurse Grant," a familiar voice said.

My eyes went straight to the person who had just walked into the room, Nurse Clarke. The same nurse who helped me when I had an abortion. I was so happy to see her face.

"My sweet Kei, what did you get yourself into gal?" Nurse Clarke held me in her arms and slowly rocked me back and forth. I don't know when I fell asleep.

* * *

I OPENED MY EYES AND WHEN MY EYES ADJUSTED TO THE light I looked around, and Nurse Clarke was setting up my food.

"You need to eat mi dear," she placed the food in front of me.

"Nurse Clarke, I need to see my boyfriend, Jaylanni. Where is he?" My voice trembled.

"Eat first, you need to feed your baby, sweetie," she patted my back.

I forced myself to eat. I wanted to make sure my unborn child was good, but I really needed to see Jaylanni.

I looked at Nurse Clarke, "How bad is he?"

She hesitated, "He was shot five times in the upper torso, he is lucky to be alive, dear. The bullets grazed his major organs, and one of the bullets caused some serious damage but his surgery went well. God will protect and heal him, sweetie. Mark my words. Dat man is a fighter. He is your soulmate, Kei'na. God was protecting you too honey because two bullets grazed your arm, and you suffered from a minor head trauma after hitting your head in your truck. Have faith and trust God."

So that's why my arm is bandaged up. I was in tears listening to Nurse Clarke. My Jaylanni... my poor man was going through this because of me.

"May I see him now, Nurse Clarke?"

"Yes, yes I will take you now." Nurse Clarke put me in the wheelchair that was in my room and wheeled me down the long hall and into an elevator. We went to the top floor, and my heartbeat was rapid as she pushed me down another hall.

She stopped in front of a room and looked at me. "Be strong mi dear."

Nurse Clarke pushed me inside the room, and I started choking up seeing Jaylanni all wrapped up and attached to all these different machines.

She pushed me closer to his bed, then she stepped back into the hallway to give us our privacy.

I held his hand, "Baby, you are going to be alright. I promise. Please be strong and keep fighting, baby. We have a long life to live together. I love you, Jaylanni. You have to be here to see our baby grow up."

My eyes opened wide when I felt him squeeze my hand weakly after I mentioned our baby. Then his eyes slowly opened.

"Nurse!" I screamed.

"Is everything okay?" Nurse Clarke rushed into the room.

"He squeezed my hand and opened his eyes, nurse!" I said excitedly.

Nurse Clarke's arms went into the air as she looked up, "God is good."

Jaylanni looked at me, and the tears were forming in his eyes. He tried to talk.

"Just relax, baby, don't say anything. I'm right here." I rubbed the back of his hand.

"This is the first time he opened his eyes since you two first came to the hospital three weeks ago." One of the nurses who joined us in the room said.

Three weeks? We were probably in a coma. I had no idea it had been that long. For the first time since waking up in the hospital, I thought about Sincere. *Where the fuck is that fuck nigga?*

I was going to ask Nurse Clarke as soon as we were alone because I didn't want these other people to hear my business.

The doctor came in and asked us to leave the room for a little bit, so that they can tend to Jay. I did not want to leave his side, but I had to let the doctor and nurses do their job.

Nurse Clarke saw the look on my face and told me that as soon as she gets the okay, she will bring me right back up here to be with my man.

We made it back to the room, and she helped me get back into the bed.

"Oh dear, before I forget. A woman has been coming here every day to see you. I think her name is Seena..." Nurse Clarke said mispronouncing Siana's name.

"My best friend, Siana."

I was so happy to know that Siana was coming to check on me. I was going to call her as soon as I had some alone time.

"Nurse Clarke, um the guy who shot us... do you know what happened to him?

"Oh no, sweetie, they can't find the shoota. I think a

famous rapper said he came home and found you and your mon shot up. He told the reporters that when he found you two, he called the police right away."

What the fuck, so this nigga wasn't locked up for shooting us! I was furious. He lied and said he found us shot up at his mansion. He knew that if he had told the police that he found Jay and me fucking in his home he would be the prime suspect. Of course, *Superstar Sincere* couldn't ruin his career or reputation, but he was willing to fuck over everyone else.

We heard a knock at the door and we both turned to see who it was. Two police officers walked in.

"Hello Ms. Konners, we would like to speak to you about the shooting," the Black officer stated.

"Hi, okay." I looked at Nurse Clarke, and she nodded her head and stepped out of the room.

Shit, it was now or never. I could name the real shooter and deal with the public scrutinizing Jay and myself, or I can keep quiet and act like I don't remember what happened or who the shooter was.

Fuck that! Sincere could have killed all three of us. My baby, Jay, and me. I was going to get justice for all of us. I just hoped that Jay would approve of my decision.

CHAPTER 29

*S*incere's face was all over the internet, TV, newspapers, magazines, and anywhere else imaginable. This is the biggest scandal he had ever experienced publicly, and the world was going insane knowing that their favorite rapper was involved in a shooting. He was named the shooter who shot his *girlfriend* and his right-hand man. Every blog and news station were racking their brains trying to put the pieces together and figure out what led to the shooting.

I was getting offered money left and right for interviews, but I wasn't going to say shit. I didn't even tell the police all of the details that led up to that moment. Folks on the internet were already speculating and making up their own stories about the situation, so I let them. Sincere was finally behind bars and that's all that matters.

A little over a month had gone by since the shooting and Jaylanni was getting stronger and stronger. I was allowed to leave the hospital, but I should've stayed there to continue to be there with Jay every day. I think knowing he was soon going to be a father was motivating him to fight hard to recover. Nurse Clarke was heaven-sent, and Jay fell in love with the elderly woman just as much as I have. She was like the sweet grandmother that we never had. She made sure that we were good 24/7. I didn't want to be alone in my big ass condo, so I had Siana, Zay and Zaliya move in temporarily until Jay was released from the hospital. Even Nurse Clarke came to my place every day.

I sat on the edge of my bed and watched the news as videos of Sincere getting released from prison appeared on my television screen. My heart sank. *How can he be getting out of jail?* I was shaking and crying when Siana and Nurse Clarke walked in. They turned off the television and sat next to me on the bed. We were all in tears as they held me.

"He's going to get what's coming to him, Kei. Don't worry mi dear," Nurse Clarke said.

"Right, karma will get his ass," Siana said, angrily.

I was an emotional wreck and needed to see Jay.

"Thank you, ladies. I love you guys so much."

I hugged them and went into my bathroom. I quickly showered and threw on some blue fuzzy sweats, with the matching fuzzy hoodie and my blue fur slides. I put my hair in a messy bun and threw on my big shades.

"I'm going to ride with you to the hospital, mi dear," Nurse Clarke said as I was getting ready to head out the door.

* * *

I WALKED INTO JAY'S HOSPITAL ROOM, AND HE WAS UP standing at the window, looking outside.

"Baby, you're up!"

I rushed over to him eagerly. He was still fragile, so I

carefully wrapped my arms around him and we embraced in a hug.

The look on his face told me that he was happy to see me too. He kissed my forehead and stared into my eyes.

"I love you, beautiful," he said slowly.

"I love you too, baby."

Jay's hands slowly went under my hoodie and he rubbed my belly. I looked at him and tears were running down his cheeks. It made me tear up too. I helped him get back in bed, and I hopped in too. We were knocked out until I felt someone's hand rubbing my leg.

I jumped up and looked to see what was on my leg, and that's when I stared into Sincere's eyes. He'd snuck in the hospital incognito style, wearing a large baseball cap, a large black hoodie, and black sweats.

Fuck! Fuck! Fuck! How the fuck did his ass get in here?

Jay turned around and his eyes flew open. He looked at Sincere with hatred in his eyes.

"Get the fuck outta here, muthafucka!" Jay said through gritted teeth.

"Nigga, shut the fuck up. Y'all fucking lucky I didn't put bullets in y'all fucking head. Jaylanni, you were my boy, man, and you chose this hoe bitch over me? Fuck loyalty, huh? Keiko ain't nothing but a gold diggin' THOT. Y'all don't think I didn't see y'all stupid asses fuckin' all over my fuckin' mansion. Jay, you really couldn't wait to get your hands on my fine ass bitch. There are hidden cameras installed all over my goddamn house. I didn't kill y'all the first time, but trust me when I say the next time, I won't miss." Sincere quickly left as fast as he came in.

Jay stiffened up and I could tell he was beyond angry.

"As mad as I am too, babe, you gotta calm down. We

need you to get better, so you can come home. Fuck Sincere."

"Baby, I promise you as soon as I'm healed, that mutha-fucka gon' see me," he threatened.

My man was serious as fuck. I just wanted Sincere to be out of our lives forever.

* * *

I COULDN'T SLEEP AFTER SINCERE'S THREAT, BECAUSE I SAW first-hand how far he would go to make sure our lives were destroyed. Nurse Clarke walked in to check on us before she clocked out.

"Do you need anything, sweetie?" she asked in a concerned tone.

"No, thank you, ma'am," my mind was running wild.

"You look frightened, gal... Are you okay?" Nurse Clarke came over to me and checked my vitals.

"I'm a little scared, Nurse Clarke."

"Was dat him, the mon dat just left?"

"Who?"

I knew exactly who she was talking about, but I didn't want to get this sweet woman involved in this mess.

"Di mon who shot you and Jay?" She waited to hear my response.

"Yes, ma'am." I looked down, embarrassed that I was involved in this scandal.

Nurse Clarke's eyes opened wide, "Why didn't you call fi help? Are you and Jay okay?"

She walked around us looking to make sure we were good. When she realized that we were okay, she calmed down.

"I will tell everyone…No more visitors for Jay. We can't risk it."

"Thank you, Nurse Clarke. What would I do without you?" I asked genuinely.

"Don't worry about that, sweetie. I will always be right here with you guys," she hugged me and exited the room.

CHAPTER 30

3 MONTHS LATER

THINGS WERE SLOWLY GETTING BACK TO NORMAL. MY MAN was home with me, and we decided that he should live in the condo with me instead of his place in Rancho Cucamonga. I could trust him with my life, so I finally let my guard down. It's a miracle that he is alive and doing as good as he is. I thanked God every day for that blessing. He wasn't a hundred percent healed yet, but he was surely getting there with the help of therapy.

My belly was just starting to protrude, and Jay couldn't get enough of it. He rubbed, kissed, and talked to my belly all day long. Siana, Zay, Zaliya, and Nurse Clarke were living with me, and I couldn't be happier. Everyone that I love all living under one roof is all that I need.

As for Sincere's punk ass, I don't know how the fuck this nigga beat his case and how fast it all went away like Jay and myself were just a piece of trash, but I guess that's why they say money talks. He walked away free from all charges, and it broke my heart tremendously. He was always the topic on gossip sites whether it was for showing off his exotic looking bitches, flossing money, or living the high-life. This world is crazy and it makes me question many things. It didn't sit right with me that this nigga was even more fucking popular for shooting us. It's like he could do no wrong in his fan's eyes. They were riding hard for a nigga they knew nothing about.

"You good, baby?" Jay snuck behind me and wrapped his arms around me.

"Yeah, babe, just thinking."

I turned around to face him, and my heart melted just staring into his eyes. I love this man so much.

"Don't be thinking too hard now."

He smiled and kissed me passionately. Kissing Jay was starting to get me moist, and I needed a quickie. He was igniting the flames between my legs. Everyone was home, but my place was so spaced out, if they were to hear me moaning, it wouldn't be too loud.

I gently pushed him on our bed and slid my hands into his basketball shorts. I rubbed his dick until it was hard. I removed my sweats, exposing my soaked pussy because I wasn't wearing panties underneath. He eyeballed me with lust. I crawled on the bed and placed my pussy on the tip of his dick and rubbed it all over before sitting on it. I moved up and down on his dick slowly as my pussy juices lubricated his dick. Jay leaned back enjoying the ride I was giving him. The more I moved up and down, the more my juices came gushing out.

"Awe shit, baby... Ride this muthafucka..."

"Mmhm, daddy... This dick feels so good..."

I started to ride a little faster, but gently because I didn't want to hurt his injuries that weren't fully healed yet.

Jay's manhood was rock hard, and I continued riding until I was cumming all over my man's dick. It wasn't too long after that his warm cum filled me up.

I collapsed right next to him out of breath. I wrapped my arm around him and we both fell asleep.

* * *

WE WERE ALL CHILLIN' AROUND THE CONDO. JAY WAS handling business on his laptop, Zay and Siana were cooking pasta for my pregnant ass, Zaliya was taking her nap, and Nurse Clarke was in the living room watching the news. I hated watching the news because it was always depressing shit being talked about, so I sat next to Nurse Clarke on my phone watching vlogs on YouTube.

"Breaking news! Rapper Sincere has been arrested for the murder of MaryAnn James," the news broadcaster announced.

My head popped up from my phone. Hearing Sincere's name got everyone's attention in the condo. Siana, Zay, and Jaylanni migrated closer to the television. Nurse Clarke hurriedly turned up the volume.

The photo of the victim appeared on the screen and I looked closely to see if I recognized the woman. *Well, I'll be damned*, it was the same woman he had sex with right in front of me for the first time in the bedroom we once shared. I had flashbacks of her smirking at me while Sincere was diggin' out her guts. Karma was definitely a bitch. I felt bad that she lost her life. She thought that she had gotten lucky and was winning; when in all actuality, she had no idea what she was getting herself into. A feeling of sadness came over me. I thought about my life. That could have been me instead of that woman.

Jaylanni walked over and wrapped his arms around me. I couldn't hold it back any longer. I broke down right there in the living room. I think that all of us were thinking the same thing, because shortly after, I felt Siana, Zay, and Nurse Clarke wrap their arms around me too. We all stood in the living room hugging with tears in our eyes.

It was a weird feeling, but at that moment, I finally felt free from Sincere knowing that he was no longer going to fuck with Jay and me. He was going to be locked up for good. People were now going to see him for the dog that he is. All of the talent that Sincere had went down the drain because he couldn't fight his demons.

His fans were piled up in front of the court building with signs that supported Sincere. There was plenty of evidence that showed that Sincere was guilty, but people were still defending him. Even with all the money in the world, this was one situation that he would not be able to get out of.

They showed clips of officers escorting Sincere out of the courtroom in handcuffs, and he looked into the camera with a scowl on his face.

I was relieved... free. Sincere was no longer going to be a problem in my life.

CHAPTER 31

*N*ews of Sincere circulated like a wildfire. It was on the news all day long. The blogs and gossip sites were going crazy talking about the murder. Sincere was probably losing his mind being locked in a jail cell. All of the fucked up shit he'd done finally caught up with his ass, and now, he was going to pay the price.

I was just happy that I didn't have to watch my back every time I went out or look over my shoulder every few seconds. All this shit was finally over, and I was going to take advantage of that. I wanted to get some fresh air, so I decided to pamper myself.

"Sisi, you wanna have a girl's day?" I asked, cheerfully.

"I wish, sis, but Zay is going out and Nurse Clarke is going to be at the hospital today, so I do not have any one to watch Zaliya."

I thought about telling her to bring the baby, but I didn't want to have Zaliya out all day, so I decided against it.

"Okay, sis. Well, I'll pick up a few things while I'm out

so that we can pamper ourselves at home. I'll set it up really nice, and we can enjoy ourselves right in the comfort of our own home." I smiled.

"Thanks, Kei, that sounds great," Siana said, enthusiastically.

"Well, I'm about to go get ready to go out."

I gave Siana and Zaliya a quick hug and went into my walk-in closet.

* * *

IT HAD BEEN A WHILE SINCE I'D GOTTEN DRESSED UP, SO I was going to get glammed up today. I put my hair in a high ponytail and added a long fake braid. I made sure my baby hairs were poppin'. I did my eyebrows, glued on my 18mm Jae Jadore mink eyelashes, and coated my lips with clear lip gloss. I wanted to keep it cute and simple. I wore a brown racerback knee length dress, and brown and white Vans. The brown color against my skin made my melanin pop, and my brown skin was glowing. My little belly was poking out in my dress and I could not help but admire that I am carrying a life inside of me. I looked in the mirror while I rubbed my belly.

Jay snuck up behind me and his hands went straight to my baby bump.

"I love you, baby," Jay leaned in and kissed my lips.

"I love you too, babe." I kissed him passionately.

The way that Jay loved me was extraordinary. I'd never experienced anything like it. He made me feel loved and made me feel special in so many ways. I was excited that our baby was made out of love; I was even happier to be carrying his seed.

"I'm about to head out for a little bit, babe."

"Do you need me to drive you?"

"No, I'll be good, babe. I'm going to go out to handle a few things and come back home as soon as I'm done."

"Okay, please be careful out there, baby," Jay said, concerned.

I never really liked going anywhere alone anymore, but I was going to put on my big girl panties and suck it up today. I needed alone time more than ever for my own sanity.

I know that I'm supposed to be pampering myself today, but I want to hit up a few baby boutiques to shop for Zaliya and my baby. We didn't know the sex of the baby yet, but I am going to get unisex items. *After I get done shopping I'll go get a facial and a prenatal massage. Then I'll go and get lunch, and head back home. I don't want to stay out all day because I don't want Jay to worry about me.*

* * *

I WALKED OUT OF THE BABY BOUTIQUE WITH BABY CLOTHES, shoes, and accessories. The owner offered to carry all of my things to my truck. Thank God they had parking spots available for pregnant women right in front of their store. I spent fifteen thousand dollars on baby items for Zaliya and my little one. They were going to have nothing but the best.

Next stop, my facial and prenatal massage. I couldn't wait for both, because it was much needed. I walked inside the facility and instantly knew that I had picked the right place. The spa had a very soothing and relaxing vibe. I was greeted right away and taken into a room that looked like a mini jungle. There were plants and beautiful flowers every-where. It sounded like I was near a waterfall from the sounds coming from the speaker placed in the room. The small framed Chinese woman guided me to the massage table and helped me get comfortable.

She started with my massage, and she would end with my facial. Her massage was firm but gentle. She was careful not to put too much pressure on my belly and I appreciated that. I was so comfortable and relaxed that I kept falling in and out of sleep. When she was finally done with my massage, she went straight to my facial.

The woman gave me a deep cleansing facial and my skin was grateful. I walked out of the spa, feeling like a brand-new woman. I was feeling great, relaxed, and in a positive mood.

I pulled up to No Reservation LA restaurant. I was craving their Belizean and Cajun cuisine. Dining alone was never my thing, but I would make an exception. I walked into the restaurant and was happy that there were only a few people scattered around enjoying their meals. I was escorted to a corner table, and it was perfect for me. I was ready to order my food as soon as I sat down.

"I'm ready to place my order. I'll get the oxtail tacos, and Cajun fries. Also, I would like a glass of water, please."

"Yes ma'am, coming right up," the waiter replied.

"Thank you." I smiled at the waiter.

I sat there waiting for my food while I read the latest gossip on the internet. After seeing Sincere's face on every website, I was no longer interested in reading the latest news. I looked around the restaurant people watching, and when the restaurant door opened, I looked to see who was coming in. In walked Samir and a White man in a business suit.

My eyes were glued to Samir. He didn't notice me sitting in the corner, but I knew that he would be able to feel my eyes on him soon. My heart was beating against my chest as I gazed at Samir's fine ass. He looked even better than I remembered. I needed to get my food and get out of this restaurant as soon as possible.

The waiter finally brought my food, and I almost told her to put everything in a to-go container, but I was too hungry to leave without eating.

I munched on my food, and my eyes were still on Samir. He sat across the room with his back facing me. It looked like he was in a business meeting from the way he was reading and exchanging documents with the White man he came in with.

The familiar feeling between my legs when Samir was around me the last time was coming back. My pussy was tingling, and I felt guilty. I tried to look around and then looked at my phone to distract myself from thoughts of Samir, but nothing was helping.

I finished my food, and when the waiter came back with my debit card, I gave her a fifty-dollar tip. As I was getting up from the table, I looked Samir's way one more time and he was looking right at me. I froze as our eyes connected. I tried to look away, but my eyes were locked with his. He looked back at the guy at his table, and quickly said something to him then got up. I almost fainted when his fine ass walked toward me.

I tried to walk away, but my legs stayed where they were. I don't know what the fuck was going on with me, but all that I know is that Samir's presence still had some type of control over me.

"Kei'na," Samir approached me and leaned in for a church hug.

"Hey, Samir," I said simply, trying to hide how I was truly feeling.

"How are you? Congratulations." He looked down at my belly.

"I'm well, thank you. How are you?"

"I'm good, Kei'na, no complaints. Just here handling business." He looked back at the gentleman who waited for him at the table.

"Happy to hear. Congrats to you as well, I read an article about you starting your business... and I saw the picture of you and your wife," I said somewhat salty, even though I had no reason to feel that way. I was the one who had ignored Samir because of his occupation.

"Thank you," he smiled.

I couldn't believe how nice he was acting after the way I ignored him the first time we went out together. It had been a while, but I don't know if I would be acting the same if someone had done that to me. It made me feel even more like shit.

"Well, I'm about to finish my meeting. I noticed you over here, and I just wanted to say hello. Take care, Kei'-na," he said, giving me another church hug before walking back to his table.

I don't know what came over me, but I stood there and stared at the back of Samir's head.

"Samir, wait," I said with hesitation.

He slowly turned around to face me, "Yes."

"Um, do you have a business card?"

I knew deep down in my heart that I should have let Samir walk away from me, but a little voice in my head told me to stop him. He stood there for a minute contemplating if he should give me his business card or not. He slowly reached into his pocket and pulled out a business card and gave it to me.

"Thank you," I said.

He nodded and slowly turned back around and walked back to his table. I quickly got myself together and rushed out of the restaurant.

I sat behind the wheel with my head leaned back as a wave of emotions took over my body. I don't know why I asked for Samir's business card, but I felt like I needed to have it. Samir is married, and I am with Jaylanni. Seeing Samir brought back memories of the way he made me feel that night on the Ferris wheel. For God's sake, I was pregnant with the man's baby, and he had no idea what I had done.

I should've trashed the business card and drove my pregnant ass home to my man who was deeply in love with me, but instead I texted the cell phone number that was printed on Samir's business card.

Me: *Hey Samir. It's Kei'na.*

I sat in the parking lot and waited for his response.

He finally texted me five minutes later. Those five minutes felt like five hours.

Samir: *What's up, Kei'na?*

Me: *It felt good seeing you.*

What I was doing was wrong, but I couldn't help myself. I guess I didn't have any self-control at that moment. After waiting for ten minutes, I still didn't get a response from Samir. I couldn't handle the waiting game, so I started my truck and left the restaurant parking lot. My mind was racing, and I felt like I was going to explode. The old Kei'na was trying to sneak out, and I was afraid. Here I was pregnant and loving Jay, but seeing Samir made me question things just that fast. I thought about the what-ifs and I just hoped that I was strong enough not to open Pandora's Box.

I made it back home and Samir still hadn't texted me

back. I was disappointed, and this should've been my sign to let it be, but I just couldn't.

Me: *I would like to meet with you whenever you have free time. I need to discuss something very important with you.*

I sat in my truck and waited to see if I would get a response. My phone buzzed and I quickly turned on the screen to see if it was him.

Samir: *Kei'na we really should just stop here before it turns into something that we will both regret.*

My heart was crushed, now here he was dismissing me.

Me: *Trust me it's nothing like that. I just really need to talk to you. Please.*

Samir: *Okay... I'm available tomorrow evening. Meet me in Beverly Hills.*

I should not have been smiling so damn hard, but I was too happy. Now, I just needed to find an excuse to get out of the house tomorrow evening. Jay wasn't really the jealous type, and he was far from controlling, but I know he would question why I was leaving especially, knowing that I did not have many friends. I couldn't tell Jay that I was going out to meet with a man that I'd fucked before. I was playing with fire, and I should've been putting this shit out, but instead I was letting this muthafucka blaze.

CHAPTER 32

I was in a good mood, and I was excited about meeting up with Samir later. I wondered if Jay felt like something was up because he kept staring at me weirdly.

"What's up, babe?"

"Nothing, my love. I just haven't seen you so happy in a while." He stared at me like he was trying to see into my soul.

"I think that massage and facial did something to my spirit, babe. I felt good getting out of the house." I partially told the truth. I just kept one little detail out.

"Well, I'm happy that you enjoyed yourself, baby. You deserve it."

I walked closer to Jay and sat on his lap facing him. I kissed him deeply, and I felt his dick rising between my legs. I knew what time it was.

I got down on my knees and pulled out his dick. Jay watched me as my head moved up and down on his rock hard wood. I spit on his dick and slurped it back up. Damn, my man's dick felt so fucking good sliding in and out of my mouth. For a minute, I wanted to text Samir and tell him never-mind, but no, I needed to have a face-to-face conversation with him.

After I was done swallowing all of Jay's cum, I winked at him as I walked into our bathroom to wash my face.

I walked back into our bedroom, "Babe, I'm going to take a drive this evening. After stepping out yesterday I realized how much getting fresh air has helped me."

"Okay, cool. I'll come with you, babe."

Shit.

"The alone time has really helped me clear my mind. How about tonight I go for a little drive and tomorrow we will go out together." I smiled at him hoping that he would agree to my suggestion.

"Alright babe, but please don't be out too late. You know it ain't safe out there for no pregnant woman."

"Okay, I won't, babe." I smiled widely on the inside.

* * *

As much as I wanted to get all dressed up, I chose to wear a tracksuit. I didn't need my man to ask why I was getting dressed up just to take a drive.

I grabbed my Telfar bag and walked to the front door. Siana and Zay were in the living room playing with Zaliya.

"I'll be back y'all," I said as I walked past them.

Siana looked at me suspiciously. I tried to look away because if anyone knows me like the back of their hand, it will be Siana. I didn't need her on my back right now, so I quickly walked out the front door.

My phone buzzed as soon as I closed the door behind me.

Siana: *You better not be up to no dumb shit, Kei.*

Fuck. Siana was too good. Her ass knew me too damn well.

Me: *Come on, sis. I'm pregnant, and you know I love Jay way too much.*

Siana: *Alright Kei, please do not do anything stupid. Be safe. Love you.*

Me: *Love you too.*

Damn, for the second time I thought about texting Samir and canceling, but I refused to do it. I was just going to talk to him and be done with it.

We agreed to meet in Beverly Hills and find somewhere secluded where we could talk. I didn't want anyone to see me and recognize me. That would be a hard one to explain to Jay, especially because I lied about where I was going.

Since Samir and I couldn't find a private area to talk, I opened up my hotel app to book a hotel room.

"I don't think that's a good idea, Kei'na," Samir mumbled.

"It will be okay, Samir. We're just going to talk and then bounce. I need to get back home soon anyway, so I'll just tell you what I need to say, then we can go our separate ways."

He got quiet and let me finish booking the hotel room. I booked a room at Mr. C Beverly Hills.

I walked into the hotel to check-in, and just my luck, the young Black girl who checked me in knows who I am. I tried to play it off and rush her ass but she was not getting the hint.

"Keiko Kei, you are my idol! OMG! Are you ever going to get back on IG? I miss seeing all of your fly ass pictures. I swear I want to be just as poppin' as you are!" she said, exuberantly.

If this girl only knew. "Thanks, hun."

I gave her a fake smile as she handed me the key card. I was in no mood to entertain some shit that I knew was fake as fuck. She had no idea what secrets hid behind those sexy pictures. I quickly left the lobby and went to the second floor to my room. I texted Samir the room number and waited for him.

Knock. Knock.

I opened the door for Samir, and it took everything in me not to jump his bones. I needed to shake this feeling fast. I was pregnant and in a relationship with Jay. After all that we've been through I couldn't do him dirty; he'd been so good to me.

"So, what's up, Kei'na? What is it that you want to talk about?" Samir cut straight to the point.

"First, I really want to apologize for ignoring you."

"No need to apologize. If that did not happen, I probably would not have met my wonderful wife." Samir smiled.

I was annoyed when he mentioned his wife, but I had no reason to be because I have someone special in my life too.

"Yeah, I guess. But I should have never treated you that way. My mindset was different back then, but trust me when I say things have changed... for the better," I said honestly.

"It's all good, Kei'na. Is there anything else? I really must get going now," he said, rushing me.

I stood there quietly giving him a look. I should've let him walk out of this hotel room forever, but I walked up to him and kissed him.

"Kei..." Samir tried to push me away, but I was persistent until he finally gave in.

Samir and I stood there in the middle of the hotel suite

kissing passionately. All thoughts of Jaylanni went out of the window. We were so caught up in the moment and before we knew it, we were both standing in the middle of the hotel suite naked.

Samir guided me toward the bed, and out of nowhere, he stopped. He turned around and looked at my stomach.

"I can't do this, Kei'na," he said, sadly.

"Samir, please. I think we both need this," I said trying to convince him. I felt like I needed to do this to find out if Jaylanni is really the man for me.

Samir was hesitant, but a minute later he guided me to the bed again. I almost stopped to tell him that I had aborted his seed, but I decided against it. This is not the time nor the place for that conversation.

After we made it to the plush bed, Samir laid me down gently. His hands slowly rubbed over my belly and found their way between my legs. Samir pushed my legs back just enough to see my clit peeking through my slit. He went down face-to-face with my pussy, and he licked my pearl tongue. I thought that I was about to explode. He started off slow and then sped up, licking my clit fast. I was quivering and squirming all over the bed. His head game was on point. I didn't know if it was a pregnant pussy thing, but my pussy was extra wet. I felt the puddle under my ass, and Samir didn't let up. He ate my pussy while I spread my legs wider for him. He was flicking his tongue and slurping up my pussy juices like I was his favorite drink.

"Oooh, shit, Samir... Damn... Fuck..." I moaned uncontrollably.

Samir kept eating my pussy until I was cumming all over the place. His face was covered in my juices. He got up to grab a towel for his face.

"Grab the condom out of my purse, please," I said to him.

Samir looked at me like he wanted to say something, but instead, he went to do what I asked.

His dick was looking good as fuck, and I couldn't wait to feel him. Thoughts of the last time we had sex flooded my mind, and I felt my pussy creaming just from the memories of him being inside me.

Samir had the condom on, and I didn't even notice because I was fantasizing about him. I was ready for him to drill my pussy something serious.

He walked back to my naked body and I spread my legs again. He slowly teased my hole with the tip of his dick. I was starting to act like an addict as I laid there feenin' for the dick that I was about to get. I could tell that Samir was being careful because of the pregnancy, and I appreciated that but I needed him to pound my insides badly. As if he heard my thoughts, I felt his dick penetrating my pussy. My eyes rolled back, as his dick went deeper inside of me.

Damn, his dick felt better than it did the night we were on the Ferris wheel. Shit, if I would have known what I know now, this nigga would've been mine.

Samir was stroking my pussy, and I couldn't stop cumming. He was fucking me like he knew my body inside out. He pulled his dick out of me and bent me over. I arched my back for him with my ass in the air. His dick slid right back inside, and Samir fucked the life out of me. He slapped my ass so hard, I knew that he had left his handprint on it. I backed my ass up on him and he fucked me faster.

"Fuck... Kei. Fuck, girl," Samir said as his nut filled the condom.

We were both breathing hard as fuck. I think reality set

in after what we just did, but there was no taking it back. We looked at each other as we heard a knock at the door. My heart was beating fast as I looked at Samir with a serious expression, and he looked back at me the same way.

"Samir, open up this motherfucking door right fucking now!" The person on the other side shouted out as they banged hard on the door.

"Samir, who the fuck is that, and how do they know you are in here?" I whispered.

"Fuck, that's my wife!" Samir was panicking, as he rushed to put on his clothes.

I was not about to get caught naked, so I rushed to throw on my clothes too. If this bitch tried to fight me, I wanted to be dressed and ready. I thought about my baby and quickly prayed that I didn't have to fight. I couldn't handle it if anything happened to my baby because of me.

"If you don't open this fucking door, I'm going to use this key that my cousin just gave me to let myself in!"

So, that's how she knew that Samir was in here. Her cousin works here and saw Samir walk in and probably followed him up to see which room he entered.

Samir looked at me sadly, and I returned the look. We had fucked up, and I finally started to feel bad. I thought about Jay, and I immediately felt nauseous. If Jay found out that I allowed another man to enter me while carrying his baby, I didn't know what would happen. Jay had never raised his voice at me or done anything to make me think that he would hurt me in any way.

How could I do this to Jaylanni? My eyes started to tear up as I thought about the consequences of my actions. I guess what Sincere had said about me a while back was true. Can't turn a hoe into a housewife.

Samir's wife had found out, but I'll be damned if my

man found out about this too. I looked over at Samir once more, and he was scratching the top of his head thinking about his next move. His wife was still banging on the door and screaming out all types of shit in the hallway. She was better than me, though; if I was her, I would've been walking through that door with no hesitation, especially if she had a key card like she claimed she had. Lord knows that I didn't want her to walk in here, but she was doing a lot of talking for a woman who just found out that her man was possibly cheating on her.

"Kei'na this will be the last time I see you. There was a time when I wanted you bad, but the feeling wasn't mutual. I'm married now, and…you're pregnant. We shouldn't have done this in the first place and now I gotta find a way to save my marriage because I know that after I walk out of this door, all hell will break loose. I don't want to expose you, so I will walk out of here before she comes in."

I seriously felt bad. For my own selfish reasons, I had ruined Samir's marriage, and I still had to go home and face my man after doing him foul. I just hoped I didn't act guilty when I got home and ended up telling on myself.

"I'm warning you one last time, Samir, bring your ass out here right now… you and fucking Keiko Kei!" Samir's wife shouted.

My eyes popped open. *Oh, fuck no, this bitch knows who her husband is in here with. This is not good!*

"Fuck, Samir, your fucking wife knows who you're in here with," I said, angrily.

Her cousin was one of those bitches at the front desk, and they must've given her my name. Samir was shaking his head from side-to-side. He grabbed his wallet off the night-stand and walked to the front door. I was going to wait inside of the room until the coast was clear to get the fuck out of dodge.

"Corrine, calm down. Let's get out of here, please," Samir calmly said to his wife when he walked out of the door.

Bam!

Samir's wife kicked the door open with so much force, it slammed against the wall and left a dent.

"Bitch, your hoe ass done fucked another woman's husband once again! I know all about your ass from social media. Samir's not on social media, but I am, so I know how you get down, bitch!" Samir's wife shouted out with her camera right in my face.

I know this stupid bitch is not recording me, fuck!

"Snapchat, here is your favorite social media THOT! In the flesh, caught red-handed with my husband."

Oh, my goodness! This bitch was recording me on Snapchat. I prayed to God that she didn't have any followers, and I prayed even harder that the people who did follow her, didn't have any connections to Jaylanni. My thoughts of leaving this fucking hotel unnoticed quickly faded away.

"Nah, bitch, show your fucking face. Be bold, just like you were bold enough to be in here with my husband alone," she kept the camera in my face.

I tried to push past her and make it out of the door, but she kept blocking me.

"And you're fucking pregnant! Samir, is this your baby?" His wife asked him, shifting her attention.

As soon as she looked at Samir, I snatched my purse off the bed and ran out of the front door.

"Corrine! Chill the fuck out!" Samir yelled at his wife.

I could hear both of them yelling at each other, as I

made my way to the stairway. I didn't have time to wait for the elevator. I needed to get as far away as possible from this hotel. My cover had been blown, and I just hoped that all of my problems would end as soon as I left the premises.

I felt my phone vibrating in my purse, but I wasn't going to check it until I made it to my truck. I jogged through the lobby, and I felt all eyes on me. Some people even had their phones out recording me. I held my head down and continued jogging in the direction of my truck.

Once I made it to my truck, I quickly pulled off leaving dust behind. After I was far enough from the hotel, I looked for a parking spot because I was shaking badly. I could hear my phone vibrating again, so I opened my purse to grab it. I looked to see who kept calling me and it was Siana. Instead of returning her missed calls, I checked the text messages that she sent me.

Siana: *Someone sent Jay a screen recording of you in a hotel with someone's husband!*

Siana: *Kei'na! How could you do that to Jay?!"*

Siana: *Answer your fucking phone!*

Siana: *I can't fucking believe you, Kei'na… I really thought you changed. Jay is going crazy right now.*

Damn, my heart dropped. Just that fast Jay knew what I had done. All of this because I wanted some dick. Samir's sex was amazing, but now I don't know if it was worth it. *Fuck my life, what have I done?*

CHAPTER 33

I drove around for two hours too afraid to go home and face Jaylanni. He hadn't even called or texted me, so I knew that I had fucked up big time. I thought about Samir and his wife. In the photo I'd seen of him and her in the article, she appeared to be one of those uppity Black chicks, but I assume that finding out that Samir was with another woman brought out the hood in her. I couldn't blame her. Samir and I had fucked up. He tried to reject me at first, but temptation was a muthafucka.

I drove around the city feeling like shit. I don't know what will happen with my relationship after this day, and if Jay left me, I don't know what I would do. I guess I should've thought about this before busting my pussy open for another man. I couldn't tell him that I had just got done getting my back blown out. He wouldn't take this shit lightly, especially because I'm carrying his child. I couldn't come up with a reason as to why I was in a hotel room with another man. Jay was no fool, so I know anything other than the truth would not work.

I drove around for another hour before I decided to take my ass back home. Siana had stopped texting and Jay still hadn't texted me, so it would be some shit as soon as I walked into my condo.

I pulled into the parking structure and sat in my truck for a few minutes. I slowly got out and walked into the lobby straight to the elevator. The ride up to my floor felt like the longest ride ever. I almost turned back around and took my ass right back down to my truck, but there was no turning back now.

I walked into my condo and there was silence. It seemed like no one was at home. I felt relieved until I heard room doors opening. The first person who walked into the living room was Siana with her hands on her hips, staring at me wildly. Next, Jaylanni walked into the living room with fire in his eyes.

"This is how you do me, Kei'na? I have done nothing but fucking love you! And to fucking top it off, you allow a nigga to fuck you with my seed inside of you!" Jay snarled.

"Kei, why?" Siana asked sadly with tears forming in her eyes.

"Anything that I say will not come out right, and I really can't explain why I did what I did. Jay, I'm so sorry baby, please, please forgive me!" I cried.

I walked up to Jay and gently grabbed his arm. He snatched his arm out of my reach.

"I'm packing my shit and leaving tonight. I can't stand to look at you, Kei'na. What you did was the ultimate betrayal, and I can't forgive you. As much as I want to fucking snap on yo ass right now, it's better for me to get the fuck outta here before I do something that I will regret later. Best believe, I'll take care of my seed, though. I'll be at every appointment, but as far as you and me, it's over Kei'-na." Jaylanni walked away.

I ran behind him, "Baby, please don't do this. I'm sorry... I'm so fucking sorry. Don't leave me, Jay. Please baby, no! We can work through this, I promise."

I was breaking the fuck down. Sobbing with snot running out of my nose. The reality of what I had done was finally sinking in, and I realized that I couldn't handle the repercussions. The only man who ever truly loved me was leaving me, and I couldn't accept it.

"Baby, don't! Don't leave us, Jaylanni!"

Everything that I said must have gone in one ear and out the other because Jay didn't even budge. I looked back at Siana. She was shaking her head with disappointment written all over her face. She rolled her eyes at me and walked back into her room closing the door behind her.

I walked into my room, and Jaylanni had already started packing his things. My heart was broken, he was really leaving me. I had fucked up big time and doubted there was anything that I could do to repair it.

"Jay, I love you, baby. I know I fucked up, but please allow me to make it right. It won't ever happen again, baby," I bawled.

Jay continued to ignore me. I looked around and almost all of his things were packed. My heart pounded against my chest. I couldn't fathom the idea of living my life without Jaylanni in it. I knew that he would be here for our baby, but the thought of there being no him and I didn't sit well with me.

Even though Samir and I connected on a level that no one else would understand, at this moment I finally knew that my heart belonged to Jaylanni. I felt bad that it took me fucking another man to realize that, but now it was too late. The damage was done.

I tried to touch Jay one more time hoping that he would tell me that he couldn't leave me, but again he pushed me away. I had hurt him in a way that I couldn't even imagine. I cannot stand here and watch the man that I love walk out of my life forever.

I walked to Nurse Clarke's room hoping that she was home.

Knock. Knock.

Her door slowly opened, and she appeared at her door. When I looked into Nurse Clarke's eyes, I could tell that she had been crying. It broke my heart even more that I had disappointed her too.

I entered her room and crawled on her bed. Nurse Clarke joined me and just held me as we both cried together.

"I'm so sorry. I'm so sorry. I'm so sorry..." I cried.

"Leave it in God's hands, darlin'. Ask for his forgiveness. I'm very disappointed, but I won't judge you, gal. Dat mon in there is a good mon, and he's hurting right now. Give him his space for a while, and you focus on yourself and dat baby growing in your belly," Nurse Clarke said as she held me close to her chest.

Nurse Clarke had grown to love Jay just like he was her son. I know it pained her that he was leaving, and it had me going crazy that I wouldn't have him holding and kissing all over me every night anymore. *Why the fuck did I do this?*

My love for dick made me lose the only man I have ever given my heart to one hundred percent. As much as I wanted to continue begging Jay to stay, I knew that I needed to take Nurse Clarke's advice and give him space.

Nurse Clarke and I continued laying there, not saying a

word. I heard the front door open, and I quickly jumped up. I barely made it, just in time to see Jaylanni walking out of the door with all of his things in tow. Fucking Samir was not worth it. I held on to my belly and fell down on the floor as the tears poured out of my eyes. I was beyond devastated. My heart crushed into tiny little pieces as I watched my man walk out of my life for good.

EPILOGUE

 *ne Year Later*

W<small>HEN</small> J<small>AYLANNI</small> <small>WALKED OUT OF MY LIFE THAT DAY, IT</small>
changed my life forever. Days after he left, I found an
engagement ring in my closet. Jaylanni was going to
propose to me. Knowing that he was never going to become
my fiancé and later my husband sucked all of the life out
of me.

Nurse Clarke has been a tremendous help, as usual.
When I feel out of it, or busy working, she is right here to
pick up the pieces when Jaylee isn't with her father. Nurse
Clarke is heaven-sent, and many days, I don't know what I
would do without her. She retired from nursing, but she
didn't want to sit around all day doing nothing so she
started volunteering at different hospitals all around Cali-
fornia. I love Nurse Clarke and would do any and everything for her. She thought that she was crowding my space,

and I felt offended when she tried to move out. I told her that I wanted her to always live with me, and I would make sure she was good no matter what. I owed that woman my life.

Siana, Zay, and Zaliya were no longer living with me and I missed having them around, but they bought a new house not too far from me. Siana was still disappointed with me, but she still helped me get through it. She said she would never turn her back on me again, and I appreciated that. Every two weeks we set some time aside to have playdates with the girls. I always looked forward to spending quality time with them. Siana and Zay were expecting again, and I am happy for them. They are having a baby boy, and I couldn't wait to meet my Godson. Being around their little family always made me miss Jaylanni even more.

Jay has been an incredible father and I love how much he loves his daughter. Even though we aren't together, I'm happy that he's been here for Jaylee while she was still in the womb, to the day she was born, and every day after that. Every time he visits her, I fight the urge to run into his arms. All of our conversations are strictly about Jaylee and that's it. I've tried to have small talk with him, but he always manages to switch the focus right back to our baby girl.

As far as Sincere, after he was found guilty and sentenced to life in prison, I never thought about him again. When they locked his ass in that cell, his die-hard fans were still riding for him and believed that he was innocent. Sincere was like a distant memory that I wanted to forget about forever.

Samir and his wife are still together from what I read in a magazine. They were posing again like a happy family with their son, and unborn baby. *Ain't that a bitch*, Samir was still in his relationship, and I had lost mine. At least one of us was happy, or so it appears.

I activated my social media accounts again, and I've been getting booked ever since. I've been working with new sponsors, modeling, booking music videos as the main girl, hosting events, and working different social media influencer gigs. I'm back to acting happy on the internet, yet deep down I feel like shit. I've been on grind mode and besides my baby girl, working has been the only thing that keeps my mind off of Jay and my fuck ups.

I am broken and empty on the inside, but all everyone sees is a young, pretty, rich girl. The only thing that is keeping me going is my baby girl, Jaylee Rose. She's such a beautiful happy baby, but every time I look into her eyes, my heart breaks because I took away the family life that she deserves. Jaylee will not be able to grow up seeing her mom and dad in love with each other and showering her with love as a family. Even though I'm suffering from depression, I try my hardest to be the best mom that I can be for her. I love Jaylee Rose with everything in me.

Being an Insta-Baddie isn't as fun as it used to be once upon a time. Now, I am just making a living trying to feed my daughter and making sure she will always be straight. Niggas are still flossing their money, cars, houses, and all the luxury shit they have, but none of that shit entices me anymore. They are steadily trying to get my attention on the internet by telling me what they could do for me, but I ignore all of those DMs. The Galores even tried to get back in contact with me for another *contract deal*, but I declined the offer. I've realized that not all money is good money, and all that glitter is not gold.

And last but not least, your girl had needs, but instead of fucking around with different niggas like I used to, I was putting my fingers to good use. I must say my fingers are strong as fuck now. Honestly, the only man that I want to have inside me is Jaylanni, but that ship has sailed. Whenever he comes around to spend time with Jaylee, I make sure to look extra sexy. I can tell he tries not to look at me, but I always catch him taking a peek. It makes me feel some type of way, but it's still not the reaction that I'm looking for. I miss that man dearly, and I would do anything to get him back. I have hope that one day we will work it out.